REBECCA OF SUNNYBROOK FARM

The Child

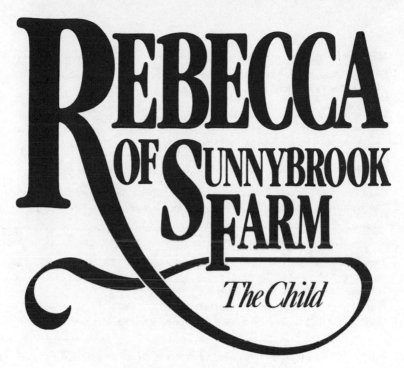

REBECCA OF SUNNYBROOK FARM

The Child

Rewritten and
re-told for today's reader

Eric Wiggin
Kate Douglas Wiggin

Illustrated by Joe Boddy

Wolgemuth & Hyatt, Publishers, Inc.
Brentwood, Tennessee

Text ©1990 by Eric E. Wiggin. All rights reserved
Illustrations © 1990 by Joe Boddy
Published April 1990. First Edition
Printed in the United States of America
96 95 94 93 92 91 90   8 7 6 5 4 3 2 (Second Printing, October 1990)

Wolgemuth & Hyatt, Publishers, Inc.
1749 Mallory Lane, Suite 110, Brentwood, Tennessee 37027

Library of Congress Cataloging-in-Publication Data

Wiggin, Eric E.
   Rebecca of Sunnybrook Farm — the child.

   Summary: Moving to the brick house in Riverboro in the 1880s to live with her maiden aunts, ten-year-old Rebecca encounters many adventures and discovers the joy of a relationship with Christ.
   [1. Aunts — Fiction. 2. New England — Fiction.
3. Christian life — Fiction] I. Wiggin, Kate Douglas
Smith, 1856-1923. II. Wiggin, Kate Douglas Smith,
1856-1923. Rebecca of Sunnybrook Farm. III. Title.
PZ7.W6376Re 1990   [Fic]   90-12176
ISBN 0-943497-95-7

To Debbie, a daughter of Maine,
who dutifully typed the final
draft for her fussy father

and

to Dot, her mother,
who toiled with me to bring this
project to its happy fruition

CONTENTS

1

WE ARE SEVEN

T he old stagecoach rumbled along the dusty road from
Maplewood to Riverboro. The day was as warm as
midsummer, though it was only the middle of May, and
Mr. Jeremiah Cobb was going as easy on his sweating
horses as possible, yet never forgetting that he carried the
mail. The hills were many and steep, and the reins lay
loosely in his hands as he lolled in his seat. He extended
one foot and leg luxuriously over the dashboard and pulled
his brimmed hat of worn felt nearly over his eyes as the
horses kept up a steady trot.

One passenger rode in the old Concord coach—a
small, dark-haired person in a glossy buff calico dress. She
was so slender and her dress starched so stiffly that she
slid from place to place on the shiny leather cushions,
though she braced herself against the middle seat with her
feet and extended her cotton-gloved hands on each side to
maintain her balance. Whenever the wheels dropped
deeply into a rut or jolted suddenly over a stone, she
bounced involuntarily into the air, came down again,
pushed back her funny little straw-and-porcupine-quill hat,
and picked up or settled more firmly a small pink parasol,
which seemed to be her chief responsibility. She also

clutched a bead purse, into which she looked whenever the condition of the roads would permit, finding great apparent satisfaction that its precious contents neither disappeared nor grew less.

Perched solidly on his bench behind the horses, Mr. Cobb guessed nothing of these harassing details of travel, his business being to carry people to their destinations, not necessarily to make them comfortable on the way. Indeed, he had forgotten the very existence of his one, quiet little passenger.

        ᴥ   ᴥ   ᴥ

When he was about to leave the post office in Maplewood that morning, a woman had jumped from a wagon, and, coming up to him, asked whether this were the Riverboro stage and if he were Mr. Cobb. He said that he was, and she nodded to a child who was eagerly waiting for the answer and who ran toward her as if she feared to be a moment too late. The child might have been ten or eleven years old, perhaps, but whatever the number of her summers, she had an air of being small for her age. Her mother helped her into the stagecoach, deposited a bundle and a bouquet of lilacs beside her, then helped the driver rope an old leather trunk on behind, and finally paid the fare, counting out the silver coins with great care.

"I want you to take her to my sisters in Riverboro," she said. "Do you know Miranda and Jane Sawyer? They live in the brick house just on the edge of the village."

"Bless your soul, I know 'em as well as if I'd made 'em," Mr. Cobb exclaimed.

"Well, she's going there, and they're expecting her. Will you keep an eye on her please?" Then turning to the child, the mother murmured, "Good-by, Rebecca. Try not to get into any mischief. And sit quiet so you'll look neat an' nice when you get there. Don't be any trouble to Mr.

Cobb." To the stagecoach driver, the lady said, "You see, she's sort of excited. We came on the train from Temperance yesterday, slept all night at my cousin's, and drove in the wagon from her house—eight miles it is—this morning."

"Good-by, Mother. Don't worry. You know, it isn't as if I hadn't traveled before."

The woman gave a short, knowing laugh and said in an explanatory way to Mr. Cobb, "She's been to Wareham and stayed overnight. That isn't much to be journey-proud about!"

"It *was traveling,* Mother," said the child eagerly. "It was leaving the farm and putting up lunch in a basket, and a little riding in the buggy, and a little ways on the steam train. And we carried our nightgowns."

"Don't tell the whole village about it, if we did," said the mother, interrupting the reminiscences of this experienced young traveler. "Haven't I told you before," she whispered, in a last attempt at discipline, "that you shouldn't talk about nightgowns and stockings and things like that, in a loud tone of voice, and especially when there're menfolk around?"

"I know, Mother, I know, and I won't. All I want to say is"—here Mr. Cobb gave a cluck, slapped the reins, and the horses started sedately down the road—"all I want to say is that it is a journey when"—the coach was really under way now, and Rebecca had to put her head out of the window over the door to finish her sentence—"it *is* a journey when you carry a nightgown!"

The objectionable word, uttered in a high treble, floated back to the offended ears of Mrs. Randall, who watched the stagecoach out of sight, gathered up her packages from the bench at the store door, and stepped into the wagon that had been standing at the hitching post. As she turned the horse's head toward home, she rose to her feet for a moment, and shading her eyes with her hand, looked at a cloud of dust in the distance.

Miranda'll have her hands full, I guess, she said to herself. *But I shouldn't wonder if it'll be the making of Rebecca.*

          ﻉﻉﻉ

All this had been half an hour ago, and the sun, the heat, the dust, and thoughts of errands to be done in Milltown had lulled Mr. Cobb's mind completely to sleep as to his promise of keeping an eye on Rebecca.

Suddenly he heard a small voice above the rattle and rumble of the wooden wheels and the creaking of the stiff leather harness. At first he thought it was a cricket, a tree toad, or a bird, but having determined the direction from which it came, he turned his head over his shoulder and saw a small shape hanging as far out of the window as safety would allow. A long black braid of hair swung with the motion of the coach; the child held onto her hat with one hand and with the other made futile attempts to poke the driver with her folded parasol.

"Please let me speak," she called.

Mr. Cobb drew up the horses obediently.

"Does it cost any more to ride up there outside with you?" she asked. "It's so slippery and shiny down here, and the coach is so much too big for me, that I rattle 'round in it till I'm almost black and blue. And the windows are so small I can only see pieces of things, and I've 'most broken my neck stretching around to find whether my trunk has fallen off the back. It's my mother's trunk, and she's very proud of it."

Mr. Cobb waited until this flow of conversation, or more properly speaking, this flood of criticism, had ceased, and then said jocularly, "You can come up here if you want to. There ain't no extry charge to sit side o' me."

"Please let me speak," she called.

So he helped her out, boosted her up to the front seat, and returned to his own place.

Rebecca sat down carefully, smoothing her dress under her with painstaking precision, and put her parasol under her skirt's extended folds between the driver and herself. This done, she pushed back her hat, pulled up her darned white knitted cotton gloves, and said delightedly, "Oh, this is better! This is like traveling! I am a real passenger now. Down there I felt like our setting hen when we shut her up in a coop. I hope we have a long, long ways to go!"

"Oh, we've only just started on it," Mr. Cobb responded genially. "We've got more'n two hours to go."

"Only two hours," she sighed. "That'll be half past one. Mother will be at Cousin Ann's, the children at home will have had their dinner, and Hannah will have done the dishes. I have some lunch, because Mother said it would be a bad beginning to get to the brick house hungry and have Aunt Miranda have to get me something to eat the first thing. It's a marvelous day, isn't it?"

"It is, certainly. Too hot, almost. Why don't you put up your parasol?"

She extended her dress still farther over her precious possession as she said, "Oh, dear, no! I never put it up when the sun shines. Pink fades awfully, you know, and I carry it to church only on cloudy Sundays. Sometimes the sun comes out all of a sudden, and I have a dreadful time covering it up. It's the dearest thing in life to me, but it's an awful care."

At this time, the thought gradually sank into Mr. Jeremiah Cobb's mind that the child perched by his side was a bird of a very different feather from those to which he was accustomed in his daily drives. He put the horse-whip back in its socket, took his foot from the dashboard, pushed his hat back, and, having thus cleared his mental decks for action, he took his first good look at the passenger, a look which she returned with a grave, childlike stare of friendly curiosity.

Driver and young passenger rolled onward over the spring countryside of New England together. Fresh were the fields and the trees in new .bud. Fresh, too, was their acquaintance. Neither could have guessed that, just as the summer was growing upon them, their relationship with each other would grow and mature. The lonely, old man and the forsaken little girl would find their hearts grow larger through each other's friendship.

2

REBECCA'S RELATIONS

They had been called the Sawyer girls when Miranda, at eighteen, Aurelia, at sixteen, and Jane, at fourteen, had participated in the various activities of village life. And when Riverboro fell into a habit of thought or speech, it saw no reason for falling out of it — at any rate, not in the same century. So although Miranda and Jane were middle-aged spinsters at the time this story opens, Riverboro still called them .he Sawyer girls. But Aurelia, the middle one, had made what she called a romantic marriage and what her sisters termed a mighty poor speculation. "There's worse things than bein' old maids," they said. Whether they thought so is quite another matter.

The element of romance in Aurelia's marriage existed chiefly in that Mr. L. D. M. Randall had a soul above farming and that he was a musician. He taught the weekly singing school in half a dozen neighboring villages, and he played the violin and "called off" at dances. He taught certain awkward lads, when they were of age to enter society, the intricacies of contra dances, and he was a marked figure in all social assemblies, though conspicuously absent from town meetings and the purely masculine gatherings at the store or livery stable or barber shop.

His hair was a little longer, his hands a little whiter, his shoes a little thinner, and his manner a trifle more polished than that of his soberer mates. Indeed, the only department of life in which he failed to shine was the making of sufficient money to live on. Rather, though his meager income from teaching music would have fed his family, Lorenzo Randall had invested it — along with Aurelia's inheritance from her father, Deacon Israel Sawyer — in Colorado silver mines and California gold mines which failed, and in China-bound Yankee clippers which had not been heard from since they sailed out of Portland. And since he had mortgaged their already poor, hardscrabble farm to cover his business losses, the Randall family was very hard pressed indeed. But not having the stomach to tend animals and crops, this chore fell upon Aurelia and the children, who scratched the soil for such thin sustenance as it would yield them.

L. D. M.'s father and his twin brother had died when he was a boy, and his mother, whose only noteworthy achievement had been the naming of her twin sons Marquis de Lafayette and Lorenzo de Medici Randall, had supported herself by taking in sewing and laundry up to the very day of her death. She had often been heard to say plaintively, "I'm afraid the faculties was too much divided up between my twins. L. D. M. is awful talented, but I guess M. D. L. would have been the practical one if he'd 'a' lived."

"L. D. M. was practical enough to get the richest girl in the village of Riverboro," replied Mrs. Robinson.

"Yes," sighed his mother, "there it is again. If the twins had married Aurelia Sawyer, 'twould 'a been all right. L. D. M. was talented 'nough to *get* Aurelia's money, but M. D. L. would 'a' been practical enough to have *kept* it."

Aurelia's share of the modest Sawyer property had been put into one thing after another by the handsome and luckless Lorenzo de Medici Randall. He had a graceful and poetic way of making an investment for each of the seven new sons and daughters that blessed their union. "A birthday present for our child, Aurelia," he would say, "a little nest egg for the future." But Aurelia once remarked in a moment of bitterness that the hen never lived that could sit on those eggs and hatch anything out of them.

Miranda and Jane had virtually washed their hands of Aurelia when she married Lorenzo. The maiden sisters at home wrote to Aurelia two or three times a year and sent modest but serviceable presents to the children at Christmas, but they refused to assist L. D. M. with the regular expenses of his rapidly growing family. His last investment, made shortly before the birth of little Miranda Randall (named in a lively hope of favors from Aunt Miranda, which never came), was to buy a share in an Alaskan fur-trading venture by taking a mortgage on their small farm two miles from Temperance. Aurelia had managed the farm herself, and so it proved a home at least, however jeopardized. Here, the unsuccessful Lorenzo died, a duty some thought too long delayed, a duty which he performed on the day of baby Miranda's birth.

In this happy-go-lucky household Rebecca had grown up. It was just an ordinary family; two or three of the children were handsome and the rest plain. Three of them were rather clever, two industrious, and two commonplace and dull. Rebecca had her father's facility for music and had been his most apt pupil. She carried the soprano part by ear, danced without being taught, played the piano without knowing the notes. Her love of books she inherited chiefly from her mother, who found it hard to sweep or cook or sew when there was a novel in the house. Fortunately books were scarce, or the children might sometimes have gone ragged and hungry.

Other forces had been at work in Rebecca, and the traits of unknown forebears had been wrought into her fiber. Lorenzo was flabby and boneless; Rebecca was a thing of fire and spirit. Her father lacked energy and courage; Rebecca was plucky at two and dauntless at five. Mrs. Randall and sister Hannah had no sense of humor; Rebecca possessed and showed it as soon as she could walk and talk.

She had not been able, however, to borrow her parents' virtues and those of other generous ancestors and escape all their weaknesses. She had not her sister Hannah's patience nor her brother John's sturdy staying power. Her will was sometimes willfulness, and the ease with which she did most things led her to be impatient with hard tasks or long ones.

But whatever else there was or was not, there was freedom at the Randall farm. The children grew, worked, fought, ate what and slept where they could. They loved one another and their parents pretty well but with no tropical passion. And they educated themselves for nine months of the year, each one in his own way, following a tradition begun by their educated father when the older children were small and continued, as best she could, by Aurelia.

As a result of this method, Hannah, who could only have been developed by forces applied from without, was painstaking, humdrum, and limited. Rebecca, on the other hand, who apparently needed nothing but space to develop in and a knowledge of terms in which to express herself, grew and grew and grew, always from within outward. Her forces of one sort and another had seemingly been set in motion when she was born. Her motivation needed no daily spur but seemed to move of its own accord — toward what, no one knew, least of all Rebecca herself.

The field of the early exhibition of Rebecca's creative instinct was painfully small, and the only uses she had made of it yet was to leave eggs out of the cornbread one day and milk another, to see how it would turn out; or to part Fanny's hair sometimes in the middle, sometimes on the right, and sometimes on the left side; and to play all sorts of fantastic pranks with the children, occasionally bringing them to the table as fictitious or historical characters found in her favorite books.

Rebecca amused her mother and her family generally, but she never was counted of serious importance, and though considered "smart" and grown up for her age, she was never thought superior in any way. Aurelia's unhappy experiences with genius, which she had seen in her deceased Lorenzo, led her into a greater admiration of plain, everyday common sense, a quality in which Rebecca seemed sometimes terribly deficient.

Hannah was her mother's favorite, so far as Aurelia could indulge herself in partiality. The parent who is obliged to feed and clothe seven children on an income of fifteen dollars a month seldom has time to discriminate carefully between the various members of her brood, but Hannah, at twelve, was at once companion and partner in all her mother's problems. Hannah kept the house while Aurelia busied herself in barn and field. Rebecca was capable of certain set tasks, such as keeping the small children from killing themselves and one another, feeding the poultry, picking up chips to kindle the fire, and wiping the dishes. But she was thought irresponsible, and Aurelia, needing somebody to lean on — having never enjoyed that luxury with her gifted husband — leaned on Hannah.

Hannah showed the result of her mother's attitude somewhat, being a trifle careworn in face and sharp in manners. But she was a self-contained, well-behaved, dependable child, and that is the reason her aunts had invited her to Riverboro to be a member of their family and participate in all the advantages of their loftier position in the world. It had been several years since Miranda and Jane had seen the children, but they remembered with pleasure that Hannah had not spoken a word during the visit, and for this reason they had asked for the pleasure of her company.

Rebecca, on the other hand, had dressed up the dog in John's clothes, and being requested to get the three younger children ready for dinner, she had held them under the pump at the well and then proceeded to slick their hair flat to their heads by vigorous brushing, bringing them to the table in such a moist and hideous state of shininess that their mother was ashamed of their appearance. Rebecca's own black locks were commonly pushed smoothly off her forehead, but on this occasion she had formed a spit curl directly in the center of her brow, an ornament which she was allowed to wear a very short time only—till Hannah was able to call her mother's attention to it. She was then sent into the next room to remove it and come back looking like a "Christian." This command Rebecca interpreted too literally, because she contrived in just two minutes to fix herself in an extremely pious hairstyle, fully as startling as the first.

The remembrance of Rebecca was so vivid that their sister Aurelia's letter was something of a shock to the quiet, aging spinsters of the brick house. It said that Hannah could not possibly be spared for a few years yet, but that Rebecca would come as soon as she could be made ready. The offer was most thankfully appreciated, Aurelia wrote, and she said that the regular schooling and church privileges, as well as the influence of the Sawyer home, would doubtless be "the making of Rebecca."

3

A DIFFERENCE
IN HEARTS

I don't know as I calculated to be the making of any child," Miranda said, as she folded Aurelia's letter and laid it in the writing table drawer. "I s'posed, of course, Aurelia would send us the one we asked for, but it's just like her to palm off that wild young one on somebody else."

"You remember we said that Rebecca or even Jenny might come, in case Hannah couldn't," Jane gently pointed out.

"I know we did, but we hadn't any notion it would turn out that way," grumbled Miranda.

"She was a mite of a thing when we saw her three years ago," ventured Jane. "She's had time to improve."

"And time to grow worse!"

"Won't it be kind of a privilege to put her on the right track?" asked Jane timidly.

"I don't know about the privilege part. It'll be a considerable chore, I guess. If her mother hain't got her on the right track by now, she won't take it to herself all of a sudden."

This depressing frame of mind had lasted until the eventful day dawned on which Rebecca was to arrive.

"If she makes as much work after she comes as she has before, we might as well give up hope of ever gettin' any rest," sighed Miranda as she hung the dish towels on the barberry bushes at the side door.

"But we should have had to clean house, Rebecca or no Rebecca," urged Jane. "And I can't see why you've scrubbed and washed and baked as you have for that one child, nor why you've about bought out Watson General Store's stock of dry goods."

"I know Aurelia, even if you don't," responded Miranda. "I've seen her house, and I've seen that batch o' children, wearin' one another's clothes and never carin' whether they had 'em on right side out or not. I know what they've had to live and dress on, and so do you. That child will like as not come here with a passel o' things borrowed from the rest o' the family. She'll have Hannah's shoes and John's undershirts and Mark's socks, most likely.

"I suppose she never had a thimble on her finger in her life," Miranda went on. "But she'll know the feelin' o' one before she's been here many days. I've bought a piece of unbleached muslin and a piece o' brown gingham for her to make up into a dress—that'll keep her busy. Of course, she won't pick up anything after herself. She's probably never seen a dust cloth, and she'll be as hard to train into our ways as if she was a wild heathen child from Borneo."

"She'll make a difference," acknowledged Jane, "but she may turn out more biddable than we think."

"She'll mind when she's spoken to, biddable or not," remarked Miranda with a shake of the last dish towel.

Miranda Sawyer had a heart, of course, but she had never let it be known that she used it for any other purpose than the pumping and circulating of blood. She was conscientious, honest, economical, industrious; a regular attendant at church and Sunday school at Tory Hill Meeting House just outside Riverboro village, and a member of the Maine Missionary Society. But in the presence of all these fine, chilly virtues, you longed for warmth and love, or lacking that, one likable failing, something to make you sure she was actually alive. She had never had any education other than that of the neighborhood district school, for her desires and ambitions had all pointed to the management of the house, the farm, and her frugal investments in stocks and bonds.

Jane, on the other hand, had gone to an academy and also to a boarding school for young ladies. Like Miranda, Jane was faithful to the church; but unlike Miranda, she seemed to come home each Sunday filled with the love of Christ for her neighbors, rather than having measured righteousness by her supposed superiority over her neighbors, who might congregate at the tavern rather than the meeting house. The same Sunday sermon, in fact, which filled Jane with love and compassion for those worse off than she, would fill Miranda with contempt for their wretchedness.

Aurelia, like Jane, attended church whenever she could, though burdened with home duties. Since the little chapel in Temperance had no regular minister, she and her brood rarely attended. Like Jane, Aurelia had the advantage of an academy education, which, with the beauty which had adorned her youth, had attracted the cultured but misfitted Lorenzo to ask her hand in marriage.

Jane, too, had had the inestimable advantage of a sorrow—not the natural grief at the loss of her aged father and mother, for she had been content to let them go to their heavenly reward, but something far deeper. She had been engaged to marry young Tom Carter, who had nothing to marry on, it is true, but who was sure to have, some time or other.

Then the war between the North and the South broke out. Tom had enlisted in the infantry at Lincoln's first call. Up to that time Jane had loved him with a quiet, friendly sort of affection, and she had given her country a mild emotion of the same sort. But the strife, the danger, the anxiety of the time, set new currents of feeling in motion. Life became something other than three meals a day and the round of cooking, washing, sewing, and church-goings. Personal gossip vanished from the village's conversation. Big things took the place of trifling ones — reports came often of sons or husbands who had fallen at Bull Run or Antietam or Gettysburg. These were the sacred sorrows of wives and mothers, pangs of fathers, and husbands' self-denials. New sympathies, new desires to bear one another's burdens came with these new sorrows.

Men and women grew fast in those days of the nation's trouble and danger, and Jane awoke from the vague, dull dream she had until then called *life* to new hopes, new fears, new purposes. Then, after a year's anxiety, a year when one never looked in the newspaper without the dread and sickness of suspense, came the telegram saying that Tom was wounded. And without so much as asking Miranda's leave, Jane packed her trunk and started for the South. She arrived in time to hold Tom's hand through the hours of pain; to show him for once the heart of a prim New England girl when it is ablaze with love and grief; to put her arms about him so that he could have a home to die in. And that was all — all, but it served.

Her love for Tom and her Lord carried her through weary months of nursing — nursing of other soldiers for Tom's dear sake. She returned home a better woman, and though she had never left Riverboro in all the years that lay between, and had grown into the likeness of her sister and of all other thin, spare, New England spinsters, it was something of a counterfeit. Underneath was still the faint echo of that wild heartbeat of her girlhood. Having learned the trick of beating through loving and suffering, her poor faithful heart persisted as it lived on memories of Tom and daily meditation in the Scriptures. Yet, stifled by Miranda's overbearing ways, Jane's heart carried on its sacred operations mostly in secret.

"You're soft, Jane," said Miranda once. "You always were soft, and you always will be. If 'twan't for me keeping you stiffened up, I believe you'd leak out under the front door and into the dooryard."

❦ ❦ ❦

It was already past the appointed hour for Mr. Cobb and his coach to be lumbering down the street.

"The stage ought to be here," said Miranda, glancing nervously at the tall grandfather clock for the twentieth time. "I guess everything's done. I've tacked up two thick towels back of her washstand and put a straw mat under her slop jar. But children are awful hard on the furniture. I expect we shan't know this house a year from now."

Jane's frame of mind had become depressed and timorous, having been affected by Miranda's gloomy predictions of evil to come. The basic difference between the sisters in this matter was that while Miranda only wondered how they could endure Rebecca, Jane had flashes of inspiration in which she wondered how Rebecca could endure them. In one of these flashes, she ran up the back stairs to put a vase of apple blossoms and a red, tomato-shaped felt pincushion on Rebecca's bureau.

The stage rumbled to the side door of the brick house, and Mr. Cobb handed Rebecca out like a real lady passenger. She alighted with great circumspection, put the bunch of faded flowers in her Aunt Miranda's hand, and received her salute—it could hardly be called a kiss without injuring the fair name of that greeting.

"You needn't 'a' bothered to bring flowers," remarked that stiff and tactless lady. "The garden's always full of 'em here when it comes time."

Jane then kissed Rebecca, giving a somewhat better imitation of the real thing than her sister.

"Put the trunk in the entry, Jeremiah, and we'll get it carried upstairs this afternoon," Miranda instructed.

"I'll take it up for ye now, if ye say the word, girls."

"No, no. Don't leave the horses. Somebody'll be comin' past, and we can call 'em in."

"Well, good-by, Rebecca; good day, Miranda 'n' Jane. You've got a lively little girl there. I guess she'll be a first-rate company keeper."

The elder Miss Sawyer shuddered openly at the adjective *lively* as applied to a child, her belief being that though children might be seen if absolutely necessary, they certainly should never be heard if she could help it. "We're not much used to noise, Jane and me," she remarked acidly.

Mr. Cobb saw that he had taken the wrong tack, but he was too unused to argument to explain himself readily, so he drove away, trying to think by what safer word than *lively* he might have described his interesting little passenger.

"I'll take you up and show you your room, Rebecca," Miss Miranda said. "Shut the screen door tight behind ye, so's to keep the flies out. It ain't fly-time yet, but I want you to start right. Take your pocketbook along with ye and then you won't have to come down for it. Always make your head save your heels. Wipe your feet on that braided rug. Hang your hat and cape in the entry there as you go past."

"It's my best hat!" protested Rebecca.

"Take it upstairs, then, and put it in the closet. But I shouldn't 'a' thought you'd 'a' worn your best hat on the stagecoach."

"It's my *only* hat," explained Rebecca. "My everyday hat wasn't good enough to bring. So I've given it to Fanny."

"Lay your parasol in the entry closet."

"Do you mind if I keep it in my room, please? It always seems safer."

"There ain't any thieves hereabouts, and if there was, I guess they wouldn't make for your sunshade; but bring it along. Remember to always go up the back way. We don't use the front stairs on account o' the carpet. Be careful of the turn in the stairs, and don't catch your foot; look to your right and go in. When you've washed your face and hands and brushed your hair, you can come down; there's water in the pitcher on the table beside the bed. By and by we'll unpack your trunk and get you settled before supper. Ain't you got your dress on hind side foremost?"

Rebecca drew her chin down and looked at the row of smoked pearl buttons running up and down the middle of her flat little chest. "Hind side foremost? Oh, I see! No, that's all right. If you have seven children you can't keep buttonin' and unbuttonin' 'em all the time; they have to do it themselves. We're always buttoned up in front at our house. Mira's only three, but she's buttoned up in front, too. Mother makes all our dresses that way."

Miranda said nothing as she closed the door, but her looks were more eloquent than words.

Rebecca stood perfectly still in the center of the floor and looked about her. There was a square of straw matting in front of each article of furniture and a hooked rug beside the four-poster bed, with a fluffed-up feather mattress

fitted with coarse muslin sheets, all of which was covered
with a fringed, white dimity counterpane.

Everything was as neat as a wax candle, but the ceilings were much higher than Rebecca was accustomed to. It
was a north room, and the window, which was long and
narrow, looked out over the porch on the outhouse, a henhouse, and the barn. It was not the room, which was far
more comfortable than Rebecca's own at the farm, nor the
lack of a sunny south view, nor yet the long journey, for
she was not conscious of weariness. Nor was it fear of a
strange place, for she loved new places and courted new
sensations. Some curious blending of uncomprehended
emotions moved Rebecca to stand her parasol in the corner, tear off her hat, fling it on the bureau, and stripping
down the bedspread, she dived suddenly into the middle of
the bed with her high-buttoned shoes on and pulled the
counterpane over her head.

In a moment the door opened quietly. Knocking was a
refinement quite unknown in Riverboro, and if it had been
heard of, would never have been wasted on a child. Miss
Miranda entered, and as her eye wandered about the vacant room, it fell upon a white and tempestuous ocean of
counterpane, an ocean breaking into strange movements of
wave and crest and billow.

"*Rebecca!*"

The tone in which the word was voiced gave it all the
effect of having been shouted from the housetops. A dark
ruffled head and two frightened eyes appeared above the
white dimity bedspread.

"What are ye layin' in your good bed in the daytime
for, messin' up the feathers, and dirtyin' the pillows with
your dusty boots?"

Rebecca rose guiltily. There seemed no excuse to
make. Her offense was beyond explanation or apology.

"I'm sorry, Aunt Miranda — something came over me — I don't know what."

"Well, if it comes over you very soon again, we'll have to find out what 'tis. Spread your bed up smooth this minute, for Abijah Flagg's bringin' your trunk upstairs, and I wouldn't let him see such a cluttered-up room for anything. He'd tell it all over town."

ᔓ   ᔓ   ᔓ

When Mr. Cobb had put up his horses that night, he carried a kitchen chair to the side of his wife, who was sitting on the back porch.

"I brought a little Randall girl down on the stage from Maplewood today, Mother. She's kin to the Sawyer girls an' is goin' to live with 'em," he said, as he sat down and began to whittle. "She's the child of that Aurelia, who ran away with Susan Randall's son just before we came here to live."

"How old a child?"

"'Bout ten, or somewheres along there, an' small for her age. But land! she might be a hundred to hear her talk! She kep' me jumpin' tryin' to answer her! Of all the queer children I ever come across, she's the queerest. She ain't no beauty; her face is all eyes. But if she ever grows up to them eyes an' fills out a little, she'll make folks stare. Land, Mother, I wish't you could 'a' heard her talk."

"I don't see what she had to talk about, a child like that, to a stranger," replied Mrs. Cobb.

"Stranger or no stranger, it wouldn't make no difference to her. She'd talk to a well pump or a grindstone. She'd talk to herself rather'n keep still."

"What did she talk about?"

"Blamed if I can repeat any of it. She kept me so surprised I didn't have my wits about me. She had a little pink parasol — it kind of looked like a doll's umbrella —

'n' she clung to it like a burdock burr to a woolen stockin'. I advised her to open it up—the sun was so hot. But she said, 'No, 'twould fade,' and she tucked it under her dress. 'It's the dearest thing in life to me,' says she, 'but it's a dreadful care.' Them's the very words, and it's all the words I remember."

Here Mr. Cobb laughed aloud as he tipped his chair against the side of the house. "There was another thing, but I can't get it right, exactly. She was talkin' 'bout the circus parade and the snake charmer in a gold chariot, and, says she, 'She was so beautiful beyond compare, Mr. Cobb, that it made you have lumps in your throat to look at her.' Rebecca Randall will be comin' over to see ye, Mother, an' you can size her up for yourself. I don't know how she'll get on with Miranda Sawyer—poor little soul!"

This concern was more or less openly expressed in Riverboro, though the folks of the village, however, had two opinions on the subject. One, that it was a most generous thing of the Sawyer girls to take one of Aurelia's children in to educate; the other, that the education would be bought at a price wholly out of proportion to its value.

Rebecca's first letters to her mother seemed to indicate that she cordially agreed with the latter view of the subject.

*"Rebecca Randall will be comin' over to see ye,
an' you can size her up for yourself."*

4

REBECCA'S POINT
OF VIEW

Dear Mother,
 I am safely here at the brick house in Riverboro. My dress was not much wrinkled, and Aunt Jane helped me press it out. I like Mr. Cobb very much. He throws the newspapers straight up to the doors and never misses, even though the horses are going at a trot.

I rode outside the coach a little while, but I got inside before I got to Aunt Miranda's house. I did not want to, but thought you would like it better if I did. Miranda is such a long word that I think I will say Aunt M and Aunt J in my Sunday letters.

Aunt J has given me a dictionary to look up all the hard words in. It takes a good deal of time, and I am glad people can talk without stopping to spell. It is much eesier to talk than write and much more fun.

The brick house looks just the same as you have told us. The parler is splendid and gives you the creeps and chills when you look in the door. The furnature is ellergant too, and all the rooms, but there are no good sitting-down places exsept in the kitchen. The same cat is here, but they do not save kittens when she has them, and the cat is too old to play with. Hannah told me once you ran away with Father, and I can see it would be nice. If Aunt M would run away I think I should like to live with Aunt J. She does not hate me quite as bad as Aunt M does.

Tell Mark he can have my paint box, but I should like him to keep the red cake in case I come home again. I hope Hannah and John do not get tired doing all my chores.

Your affectionate daughter,
Rebecca

P. S. Please give this piece of poetry to John because he likes my poetry even when it is not very good. This piece is not very good, but it is true, but I hope you won't mind what is in it as you ran away.

> This house is dark and dull and dreer.
> No light doth shine from far or near.
> It's like a tomb.

> And those who live herein
> Are most as dead as serrafim,
> Though not as good.

> My gardian angel is asleep;
> At leest he doth no vigil keep.
> Oh, woe is me!

> Then bring me back to Sunnybrook Farm
> Where none alive did wish me harm.
> Dear home of youth!

P. S. again. I made the poetry like a piece in a book but could not get it right at first. You see *tomb* and *good* do not sound well together, but I wanted to say *tomb* dredfully, and sence serrafim are always *good*, I couldn't

take that out. I have made it over now. It does not say my
thoughts as well, but I think it is more right. Give the best
one to John as he keeps them in a box with his birds'
eggs. This is the best one.

Sunday Thoughts
by
Rebecca Rowena Randall

This house is dark and dull and drear.
No light doth shine from far or near
Nor ever could.

And those of us who live herein
Are most as dead as seraphim,
Though not as good.

My guardian angel is asleep.
At least he doth no vigil keep
But far doth roam.

Then bring me back to Sunnybrook Farm
Where none alive did wish me harm.
Dear childhood home!

      za.   za.   za.

(Two weeks after Rebecca first wrote her mother, she
wrote again.)

Dear Mother,

I am thrilling with unhappiness this morning. I got that
out of the book, *Cora, the Doctor's Wife*, whose husband's
mother was very cross and unfealing to her like Aunt M is
to me. I wish Hannah had come instead of me, for it was
Hannah that was wanted, and she is better than I am and
does not answer back so quick.

Are there any peaces of my buff calico? Aunt J wants
enough to make a new waist, buttoned behind so I won't

look so outlandish. The styles are quite pretty in Riverboro and those at church quite ellergant, more so than in Temperance.

> This town is stylish, gay and fair,
> And full of wealthy riches rare,
> But I would pillow on my arm
> The thought of dear, sweet Sunnybrook
> Farm.

School is pretty good. The teacher can answer more questions than the Temperance one, but not so many as I can ask. I am smarter than all the girls but one but not so smart as two boys. Emma Jane can add and subtract in her head like a streek of lightning and knows the speling book right through but has no thoughts of any kind. She is in the *McGuffey Third Reader* but does not like stories in books. I am in the *Sixth Reader*, but just because I cannot say the seven multiplication Table, Miss Dearborn threttens to put me in the baby Primer class with Elijah and Elisha Simpson, little twins.

> Sore is my heart and bent with stubborn
> pride,
> With Lijah and Lisha I am tied.
> My soul recoils like Cora Doctor's Wife.
> Like her, I feer I cannot bare this life.

I am going to try for the speling prize, but I feer I cannot get it. I would not care, but wrong speling looks dredful in poetry. Last Sunday when I found seraphim in the dictionary I was ashamed I had made it serrafim, but seraphim is not a word you can guess at like another long one outlandish in this letter which spells itself. Miss Dearborn says use the words you can spell, and if you can't spell seraphim, make angel do, but angels are not quite the same as seraphims. I sew on brown gingham dresses every afternoon when Emma Jane and the Simpsons are playing house or running on the logs in the mill pond when their mothers do not know it. Their mothers are afraid they will drown, and Aunt M is afraid I will wet my clothes, so will not let me play either. I can play from half past four to supper and after supper a little bit and Saturday afternoons.

I am glad to hear from you that our best cow at Sunnybrook has a calf and it is spotted. It is going to be a good year for apples and hay, so you and John will be glad and we can pay a little more mortgage.

Miss Dearborn asked us what is the purpose of edducation, and I said the purpose of mine was to help pay off the morgage. She told Aunt M and I had to sew extra for punishment, because she says a morgage is a disgrace like stealing or smallpox and it will be all over town that we have one on our farm. Emma Jane is not morgaged nor Richard Carter nor Dr. Winship, but the Simpsons are.

> Rise my soul, strain every nerve,
> Thy morgage to remove,
> Gain thy mother's heartfelt thanks
> Thy family's grateful love.

Pronounce *family* quick or it won't sound right.

Your loving daughter,
Rebecca

        ❧   ❧   ❧

(With the letter to her mother, Rebecca also sent one to her brother John.)

Dear John,

You remember when we tide the new dog in the barn how he bit the rope and howled. I am just like him, only the brick house is the barn and I cannot bite Aunt M because I must be grateful, and edducation is going to be the making of me and help you pay off the morgage when we grow up.

Your loving sister,
Becky

5

WISDOM'S WAYS

Rebecca's arrival had been on a Friday. On the Monday following, she began her education at the Riverboro Village School, about half a mile distant as the crow flies, or a mile by the road that led through Riverboro Village.

Miss Miranda Sawyer borrowed a neighbor's horse and wagon and drove Rebecca to the schoolhouse, interviewing the teacher, Miss Dearborn, arranging for books, and generally starting the child on a path that was to lead to boundless knowledge. Miss Dearborn had had no special preparation in the art of teaching. Like many rural Maine schoolmarms in those days, she was only a girl of seventeen, and teaching came to her naturally, so her family said. Like a beaver who builds dams because God has decreed that he must, Miss Dearborn lay, log upon log, the foundations of basic education in her pupils' minds.

Rebecca walked to school after the first morning. She loved this part of the day's program. When the dew lay not too heavy on the grass and the weather was fair and pleasant, there was a shortcut through the woods. She turned off the main road, squeezed through the split rail bars which served as a gate in Uncle Josh Woodman's barbed-wire pasture fence, waved away Mrs. Carter's cows, trod the short grass of the pasture, with its well-worn path running through gardens of buttercups and whiteweed, and groves of ivory leaves and sweet fern. She descended a little hill, jumped from stone to stone across a woodland brook which meandered toward the Saco River which bordered the fields of the brick house, and startled the drowsy frogs, who were always winking and blinking in the morning sun.

Then came the "woodsy bit," with her feet pressing the slippery carpet of brown pine needles — the "woodsy bit" so full of dewy morning surprises: fungus growths of brilliant orange and crimson springing up around the stumps of dead trees, beautiful things born in a single night, and now and then the miracle of a little clump of waxen Indian pipes, seen just quickly enough to be saved from her careless tread. Then she climbed a stile over a fence, went through a grassy meadow, slid under another set of bars, and came out into the road again, having saved nearly half a mile. How delicious it all was! Rebecca clasped her *Harvey's Grammar* and *Ray's Arithmetic* with a joyful sense of knowing her lessons. Her tin dinner pail swung from her right hand as she trod along, and she had a blissful consciousness of the two soda biscuits spread with butter and syrup, the baked cup custard, the doughnut, and the square of hard gingerbread.

Sometimes, as she skipped along, Rebecca rehearsed aloud whatever piece she was going to speak on the next Friday afternoon:

> A soldier of the Legion lay dying
> in Algiers,
> There was lack of women's nursing,
> There was dearth of woman's tears.

*She jumped from stone to stone . . . and startled
the drowsy frogs.*

How she loved the swing and the sentiment of the poem! How her young voice quivered whenever she came to the refrain: "But we'll meet no more at Bingen, dear Bingen on the Rhine." It always sounded beautiful in her ears as she sent her little treble into the clear morning air. Another early morning favorite was:

Woodman, spare that tree!
Touch not a single bough!
In youth it sheltered me,
And I'll protect it now.

When Emma Jane Perkins walked through the shortcut with Rebecca, the two girls used to render this poem with the appropriate dramatic action. Emma Jane always chose to be the woodman because she had nothing to do but raise an imaginary ax above her head. On the one occasion when she attempted the part of the tree's protector, she claimed that she felt "so awful foolish" that she refused to try it again, much to the secret delight of Rebecca, who found the woodman's role much too tame for her soaring ambition. Rebecca reveled in the impassioned appeal of the poet and implored the ruthless woodman to be as brutal as possible with the ax, so that she might properly put greater spirit into her lines. One morning, feeling more frisky than usual, Rebecca fell upon her knees and wept upon the woodman's petticoat. But she realized how silly she looked the minute she had done it.

"That wasn't right. It was silly, Emma Jane. But I'll tell you where it might come in — in 'Give me Three Grains of Corn.' You be the mother, and I'll be the famishing Irish child. For pity's sake put the ax down. You are not the woodman any longer!"

"What'll I do with my hands, then?" asked Emma Jane.

"Whatever you like," Rebecca answered wearily. "You're just a mother—that's all. What does your mother do with her hands? Now here goes.

> Give me three grains of corn, Mother,
> Only three grains of corn.
> 'Twill keep the little life I have
> Till the coming of the morn.

This sort of thing made Emma Jane nervous and fidgety, but she was Rebecca's slave and went along with the game, no matter how uncomfortable it made her.

At the last set of bars the two girls were sometimes met by a swarm of the Simpson children, who lived on the Blueberry Hill Road in a tar-paper house with a weathered door and a tumbledown barn behind. Rebecca felt pity for the Simpsons from the first because there were so many of them and their clothes were so patched and darned, just like her own family's at Sunnybrook Farm.

The little schoolhouse with its flagpole on top and its two doors in front, one for boys and the other for girls, stood on the crest of a hill at the opposite end of the village from the brick house, with rolling fields and meadows on one side, a narrow stretch of pine woods on the other to separate it from Riverboro's cluster of houses, and the Saco River glinting and sparkling in the distance. It boasted no attractions within. All was as bare and plain and sparse as it well could be, for the villages along the river expended so much money in repairing and rebuilding bridges that they were obliged to be very economical in school privileges.

The teacher's desk and chair stood on a platform in one corner. There was a cast-iron, pot-bellied stove never blackened oftener than once a year, a map of the United States, two heavy slate blackboards, a ten-quart tin pail of water and long-handled dipper on a corner shelf, and wooden desks and benches for the scholars, who only numbered twenty in Rebecca's time. The seats were higher in the back of the room, and the more advanced and longer legged pupils sat there, the position being greatly to be envied as they were not only nearer to the windows but farther from the teacher.

There were classes of a sort, although nobody, broadly speaking, studied from the same books with anybody else. Rebecca, in particular, was so difficult to classify that Miss Dearborn soon gave up the attempt altogether. She read with Dick Carter and Ted Perkins, who were preparing for high school, recited arithmetic with little Susan Simpson and geography with Emma Jane Perkins, and studied grammar after school hours with Miss Dearborn alone. Full to the brim as Rebecca was of clever thoughts and quaint fancies, she made, at first, but a poor hand at composition. The labor of writing and spelling, with the added difficulties of punctuation and capitals, interfered sadly with her expression of ideas.

She took history with Alice Robinson's class, which was attacking the subject of the Revolution, though Rebecca was instructed to begin with the discovery of America, a three hundred year lag behind her group. In a week, however, she had mastered the course of events up to the Revolution, and in ten days had arrived at Yorktown, where the class had apparently established summer quarters. Then finding that extra effort would only result in her reciting with the oldest Simpson boy, she deliberately held herself back, for wisdom's ways were not those of pleasantness nor her paths those of peace if she were compelled to tread them in the company of "Seesaw" Simpson.

Samuel Simpson was generally called "Seesaw" because of his difficulty in making up his mind. Whether it were a question of fact, of spelling, or of date, of going swimming or fishing, of choosing a book in the Sunday school library or a stick of candy at the village store, he had no sooner decided on one plan of action than his wish fondly reverted to the opposite one. Seesaw was pale, flaxen haired, blue eyed, and round shouldered. Perhaps because of his weakness, Rebecca's decisiveness fascinated him, and although she snubbed him nearly to the point of driving him crazy, he could never keep his eyes away from her.

The force with which she tied her shoe when the lacing came undone, the flirt over her shoulder she gave her black braid when she was excited, her manner of studying—book on desk, arms folded, eyes fixed on the opposite wall—all had an abiding charm for Seesaw Simpson. When she walked to the water pail in the corner and drank from the dipper, unseen forces dragged Seesaw from his seat to go and drink after her. Not only was there something akin to closeness in drinking after Rebecca, but there was the fearful joy of meeting her in the aisle and receiving a cold and scornful look from her wonderful eyes.

On a certain warm day in June, Rebecca's thirst exceeded the bounds of propriety. When she asked a third time for permission to quench it at the common bucket, Miss Dearborn nodded yes, but she lifted her eyebrows unpleasantly as Rebecca neared the desk. As Rebecca replaced the dipper, Seesaw promptly raised his hand, and Miss Dearborn wearily granted permission.

"What is the matter with you, Rebecca?" she asked.

"I had salty smoked herring for breakfast," answered Rebecca.

There seemed nothing humorous about this reply, since she had only stated a fact, but an irrepressible giggle ran through the school. Miss Dearborn did not enjoy jokes neither made nor understood by herself, and her face turned red. "I think you had better stand by the pail for five minutes, Rebecca. It may help you to control your thirst."

Rebecca's heart fluttered. She had to stand in the corner by the water pail and be stared at by all the scholars! She moved a step nearer her seat but was stopped by Miss Dearborn's command in a still firmer voice. "Stand by the pail, Rebecca! Samuel, how many times have you asked for water today?"

"This is the fourth."

"Don't touch the dipper, please. The school has done nothing but drink this afternoon. It has had no time whatsoever to study. I suppose you had something salty for breakfast, Samuel?" queried Miss Dearborn sharply.

"I had salty smoked herring for breakfast, just like Rebecca." More giggles, louder than before.

"I judged so. Stand by the other side of the pail, Samuel."

Rebecca's head was bowed with shame and wrath. Life looked too black a thing to be endured. The punishment was bad enough, but to be coupled in correction with Seesaw Simpson was beyond human endurance. Singing was the last school exercise of the afternoon, and Minnie Smellie chose "Shall We Gather at the River?" It was a deadly choice and seemed to the students to hold some secret association with the situation involving Rebecca and Seesaw. At any rate, there was apparently some reason for the energy and vigor with which the scholars shouted the chorus again and again:

> Shall we gather at the river,
> The beautiful, the beautiful river?

Miss Dearborn stole a look at Rebecca's bent head and was frightened. The girl's face was pale except for two red spots glowing on her cheeks. Tears hung on her lashes.

Her breath came and went quickly, and the hand that held her pocket handkerchief trembled like a leaf.

"You may go to your seat, Rebecca," said Miss Dearborn at the end of the first song. "Samuel, stay where you are till the close of school. And let me tell you, scholars, that I asked Rebecca to stand by the pail only to break up this habit of constant drinking, which is nothing but a desire to walk to and fro over the floor. Every time Rebecca has asked for a drink today the whole school has gone to the pail one after another. She is really thirsty, and I dare say I ought to have punished you for following her example, not her for setting it. What shall we sing now, Alice?"

"'The Old Oaken Bucket,' please."

"Think of something dry, Alice, and change the subject. Yes, 'The Star-Spangled Banner' if you like, or anything else."

Rebecca sank into her seat and pulled the songbook from her desk. Miss Dearborn's explanation had lifted some of the weight from her heart, and she felt a trifle raised in her self-esteem. As the class began to relax while singing, respectful sympathy for Rebecca's plight began to show. Ted Perkins, who could not sing, dropped a piece of maple sugar into her lap as he passed her on his way to the blackboard to draw a map of Maine. Alice Robinson rolled a new slate pencil over the floor with her foot until it reached Rebecca's seat, while her seatmate, Emma Jane, had made up a little mound of paper spitballs and labeled them "Bullets for you know who."

By the time she was alone with her teacher for her grammar lesson, Rebecca had nearly recovered her composure, which was more than Miss Dearborn had done. The last clattering foot had echoed through the hall, and Seesaw's backward glance of penitence had been met and answered defiantly by one of cold disdain.

"Rebecca, I am afraid I punished you more than I meant," said Miss Dearborn, who was only seventeen herself, and in her year of teaching country schools had never encountered a child like Rebecca.

"I hadn't missed a question this whole day, nor whispered, either," quavered the culprit. "And I don't think I ought to be shamed just for drinking."

"You started all the others, or it seemed as if you did. Whatever you do they all do, whether you laugh or write notes or ask to leave the room or get a drink. And it must be stopped."

"Sam Simpson is a copycat!" stormed Rebecca. "I wouldn't have minded standing in the corner alone — that is, not so very much — but I couldn't bear standing with him."

"I saw that you couldn't, and that's the reason I told you to take your seat and left him in the corner. Remember that you are a stranger in this village and school, and they take more notice of what you do, so you must be careful. Now let's have the conjugations. Give me the verb *to be,* potential mood, past perfect tense."

Rebecca recited, "I might have been, Thou mightst have been, He might have been; We might have been, You might have been, They might have been."

"Give me an example, please."

"I might have been glad, Thou mightst have been glad, He, she, or it might have been glad," she said without hesitation.

"'He' or 'she' might have been glad, because they are masculine and feminine, but could '*it*' have been glad?" asked Miss Dearborn, who was very fond of splitting hairs.

"Why not?" asked Rebecca.

"Because 'it' is neuter gender."

"Couldn't we say, 'The kitten might have been glad if it had known it was not going to be drowned?'"

"Ye—es," Miss Dearborn answered hesitatingly, never sure of herself under Rebecca's rapid-fire questions. "But though we often speak of a baby, a chicken, or a kitten as *it*, they are really masculine or feminine gender, not neuter."

Rebecca reflected a long moment and then asked, "Is a hollyhock neuter?"

"Oh yes, of course it is, Rebecca."

"Well, couldn't we say, 'The hollyhock might have been glad to see the rain, but there was a weak little hollyhock bud growing out of its stalk, and it was afraid that it might be hurt by the storm.' So the big hollyhock was kind of afraid, instead of being real glad?"

Miss Dearborn looked puzzled as she answered, "Of course, Rebecca, hollyhocks could not be sorry or glad or afraid, really."

"We can't tell, I s'pose," replied the child. "But *I* think they are, anyway. Now, what shall I say?"

"The subjunctive mood, past perfect tense of the verb *to know.*"

If I had known, If we had known,
If thou hadst known, If you had known,
If he had known, If they had known.

"Oh, the subjunctive is the saddest tense," sighed Rebecca with a little break in her voice. "Nothing but *ifs, ifs, ifs!* It makes you feel that if they only *had* known, things might have been better!"

Miss Dearborn had not thought of it before, but on reflection she believed the subjunctive mood was a sad one and *if* rather a sorry part of speech. "Give me some more examples of the subjunctive, Rebecca, and that will do for this afternoon," she said.

"If I had not loved smoked herring, I would not have been thirsty," said Rebecca with a smile like a rainbow as she closed her grammar book. "If thou hadst loved me truly, thou wouldst not have stood me in the corner. If Seesaw had not loved wickedness, he would not have followed me to the water pail."

"And if Rebecca had loved the rules of the school, she would have controlled her thirst," finished Miss Dearborn with a kiss on Rebecca's cheek, and the two parted friends.

6

SUNSHINE
IN A SHADY PLACE

The little schoolhouse on the hill had its moments of
triumph as well as its troubles, but it was fortunate
that Rebecca had her books and her new friends to keep
her interested and busy, or life would have gone heavily
with her that first year in Riverboro. She tried to like her
Aunt Miranda but failed in the attempt. She was a very
faulty and passionately human child with no wish to be the
angel of the house. But Rebecca had a sense of duty and a
desire to be good — respectably, decently good.

Whenever she fell below this standard, Rebecca was
miserable, for her mother had taught her from the Bible to
do good and to pray for those who despitefully use you. She
did not like to be under her aunt's roof, eating food, wearing clothes, and studying books provided by her, and yet
dislike her so heartily all the time. She felt that this was
wrong and mean, and whenever the feeling of remorse was
strong within her, she made a desperate effort to please her
grim and difficult relative. Jesus, Rebecca knew, would
have her love Aunt Miranda, but this was proving difficult

indeed. How could she succeed when she was never permitted to be herself in Aunt Miranda's presence?

The searching look of the eyes, the sharp voice, the hard knotty fingers, the thin straight lips, the long silences, the front-piece wig that didn't match her hair, the very obvious part that seemed sewed into her hair with linen thread on black net—there was not a single item about her aging aunt that appealed to Rebecca. Certain narrow, unimaginative, and autocratic grown-ups seem to call out the most mischievous and sometimes the worst traits in children. Miss Miranda, had she lived in a populous city neighborhood, would have had her doorbell pulled, her gate tied up, or dirt traps set in her garden paths. The Simpson twins stood in such awe of her that they could not be persuaded to come to the side door, even when Miss Jane held gingerbread cookies in her outstretched hands.

Needless to say, Rebecca irritated her aunt with every breath she drew. She continually forgot and started up the front stairs because it was the shortest route to her bedroom. She left the dipper on the kitchen shelf instead of hanging it up over the water pail. She sat in the chair the cat liked best. She was willing to go on errands but often forgot what she was sent for. She left the screen doors ajar, so that flies came in. Her tongue was ever in motion; she sang or whistled when she was picking up chips. She was always messing with flowers, putting them in vases, pinning them on her dress, and sticking them in her hair. Finally, she was an everlasting reminder of her father, thought worthless and foolish by Miranda. His handsome face and engaging manner had deceived Aurelia, Rebecca's mother, Miranda had on more than one occasion hinted.

Now if Hannah had come to live at the brick house—Hannah took after the other side of the family—she was "all Sawyer." Hannah spoke only when spoken to, instead of first, last, and all the time. Hannah was a member of the church. Hannah liked to knit. Hannah was probably, or would have been, a pattern of all the smaller virtues. But instead of Hannah, here was this black-haired, gypsy-like daughter of a French Canadian, with eyes as big as cart-wheels, installed as a member of the household.

What sunshine in a shady place was Aunt Jane to Rebecca! Aunt Jane with her quiet voice, her understanding eyes, her ready excuses to Miranda in those first difficult weeks, when the impulsive little stranger was trying to settle down into the brick house ways. She did learn them, by degrees, and the constant fitting of herself to these new and difficult standards of conduct seemed to make her older than ever for her years.

She took her sewing and sat beside Aunt Jane in the kitchen while Aunt Miranda kept her post of observation of the affairs in the village street at the sitting room window. Sometimes they would work on the side porch where the clematis and woodbine shaded them from the hot sun. To Rebecca the yards of brown gingham cloth seemed to continue forever. She made hard work of sewing—broke her thread, dropped her thimble into the syringa bushes, pricked her finger, wiped the perspiration from her forehead, could not match the checks, puckered the seams. She polished her needles to nothing, pushing them in and out of the emery strawberry pincushion, and she waxed them with beeswax, but still they squeaked. Aunt Jane's patience held good, and some small measure of skill was creeping into Rebecca's fingers, fingers that held pencil, paintbrush, and pen so cleverly, yet were so clumsy with the dainty needle.

When the first brown gingham jumper was completed, the child seized what she thought an opportune moment and asked her Aunt Miranda if she might have another color for the next one.

"I bought a whole piece of the brown," said Aunt Miranda flatly. "That'll give you two more dresses with plenty for sleeves and to patch and let down with as you grow, an' it'll be more economical."

"I know. But Mr. Watson says he'll take back part of it and let us have pink and blue for the same price."

"Did you ask him?"

"Yes'm."

"It was none o' your business."

"I was helping Emma Jane choose cloth for aprons, and I didn't think you'd mind which color I had. Pink keeps clean just as nice as brown, and Mr. Watson says it'll wash without fading."

"Mr. Watson's a splendid judge of laundry, I guess. I don't approve of children bein' rigged out in fancy colors, but I'll see what your Aunt Jane thinks."

"I think it would be all right to let Rebecca have one pink and one blue gingham," said Jane. "A child gets tired of sewing on one color. It's only natural she should long for a change. Besides, she'd look like a charity child, always wearin' the same brown with a white apron. And it's dreadful unbecomin' to her!"

"Handsome is as handsome does, say I. Rebecca never'll come to grief because of her beauty, that's certain, and there's no use in humoring her to think about her looks. I believe she's vain as a peacock now, without anything to be vain about," snapped Miranda.

"She's young and attracted to bright things — that's all. I remember well enough how I felt at her age."

"You was considerable of a fool at her age, Jane."

"Yes, I was, thank the Lord! I only wish I'd known how to take a little of my foolishness along with me, as some folks do, to brighten my declining years."

There finally was a pink gingham jumper, and when it was nicely finished, Aunt Jane gave Rebecca a delightful surprise. She showed her how to make pretty trimming of narrow white linen tape by folding it in pointed shapes and sewing it down very flat with neat little stitches.

"It'll be good fancy work for you, Rebecca, for your Aunt Miranda won't like to see you always reading in the long winter evenings. Now if you think you can baste two rows of white tape 'round the bottom of your pink skirt and keep it straight by the checks, I'll stitch them on for you with the sewin' machine and trim the waist and shoulder straps with pointed tape trimming, so the dress'll be real pretty for second best."

Rebecca's joy knew no bounds. "I'll baste like a house afire!" she exclaimed. "It's a thousand yards 'round that skirt, as well I know, having hemmed it. But I could sew pretty trimmin' on if it was from here to Milltown. Oh, do you think Aunt Miranda'll ever let me go to Milltown with Mr. Cobb? He's asked me again, you know. But one Saturday I had to pick strawberries, and another it rained, and I don't think she really approved of my going. It's *twenty-nine* minutes past four, Aunt Jane, and Alice Robinson has been sitting under the currant bushes for a long time waiting for me. Can I go and play?"

"Yes, you may go, and you'd better run as far as you can out behind the barn, so your noise won't distract your Aunt Miranda. I see Susan Simpson and the twins and Emma Jane Perkins hidin' behind the fence now."

Rebecca leaped off the porch, snatched Alice Robinson from under the currant bushes, and what was much more difficult, succeeded by means of a complicated system of signals in getting Emma Jane away from the Simpson children and giving them the slip altogether. They were much too small for certain pleasurable activities planned for that afternoon. But they were not to be despised, for the Simpson family had the most fascinating dooryard in the village. In it, in bewildering confusion, were old sleighs, heavy, horse-drawn logging pungs, horse rakes, hogshead barrels, settees without backs, bedsteads without heads in all stages of disability, and never the same collection on two consecutive days.

Mrs. Simpson was seldom at home, and even when she was, she had little concern for what happened on the premises. A favorite game of the neighborhood children was to make the house into a fort, gallantly held by a handful of American soldiers against a besieging force of the British army. Great care was used in choosing sides, for the children would let nobody win but the Americans. Seesaw Simpson was usually made commander-in-chief of the British army, and a weak and uncertain one he was, capable, with his contradictory orders and his fondness for the extreme rear, of leading any regiment to an inglorious death. Sometimes the long-suffering house was a log hut, and the brave settlers defeated a band of hostile Indians, or occasionally were massacred by them. But in either case, the Simpson house looked, to quote a Riverboro expression, "as if the devil had been having an auction in it."

The "secret spot" was second only to the Simpson home as the children's favorite playground. There was a velvety stretch of ground in the old Sawyer pasture, now vacant of cows. It was full of fascinating hollows and hillocks, as well as verdant levels, on which to build playhouses. A group of trees concealed it from view and flung a grateful shade over the dwellings erected there by Rebecca and her cronies.

It had been hard yet sweet labor to take armfuls of board edgings and slabwood from the sawmill by the river to this secluded spot, mostly after supper in the dusk of the evenings. Here in wooden soap boxes hidden among the trees were stored all their treasures. Tiny baskets and plates and cups made of burdock burr balls there were, bits of broken china for parties, dolls, soon to be outgrown but serving well as characters in all sorts of romances enacted there.

A tall, square house of wooden board edgings was to be built around Rebecca this very afternoon, and she was to be an unfortunate and wrongly jailed inmate, leaning against the bars of her prison. It was a wonderful experience standing inside the building with Emma Jane's apron wound about her hair as a kerchief; wonderful to feel that when she leaned her head against the wooden bars they seemed to turn to cold steel; wonderful that her eyes were no longer Rebecca's but mirrored something of the prisoner's hapless woe.

"Ain't it lovely?" sighed the girls, who had done most of the work, as they admired the result of their labors.

"I hate to take it down," said Alice. "It's been such a sight of work."

"If you think you could move up some stones and just take off the top rows, I could step over," suggested Rebecca. "Then leave the stones, and you two can step down into the prison tomorrow and be the two little princes in the tower, and I can murder you."

"What princes? What tower?" asked Alice and Emma in one breath. "Tell us about them."

"Not now," said Rebecca firmly. "It's my supper time."

"It would be elergant being murdered by you," said Emma Jane loyally, "though you are awful mean when you murder. Or we could have Elijah and Elisha for the princes."

"They'd yell when they was murdered," objected Alice. "You know how silly they are at plays, all except Clara Belle. Besides, if we once show them this secret place, they'll play in it all the time, and perhaps they'd steal things, like their father."

"They needn't steal just because their father does," argued Rebecca. "And don't you ever talk about it before them if you want to be my secret, partic'lar friends. My mother tells me never to say hard things about people's own folks. She says it's wicked to shame people for what isn't their fault."

7

RIVERBORO SECRETS

Mr. Abner Simpson spent little time with his family, since his rather unorthodox methods of horse trading, or swapping of farm implements, furniture, and vehicles of various kinds — deals with which his customers were never long pleased — usually ended in his passing a longer or shorter term in jail, according to the disposition of the judge and the anger of the aggrieved. For when a poor man without goods or property has the incurable habit of swapping, it follows naturally that he must have something to swap. But having nothing of his own, and not usually putting a great deal of his profits back into his business, it follows still more naturally that he must swap something belonging to his neighbors.

Mr. Simpson was absent from the home circle at the moment because he had exchanged the Widow Rideout's sleigh for Joseph Goodwin's plow. Goodwin had recently moved to Riverboro and had never before met the urbane and persuasive Simpson. Goodwin's plow Simpson speedily traded with a man "over Wareham way," and he got in exchange for it an old horse which his owner did not need, since he was leaving town to visit his daughter for a year. The Wareham citizen had arranged with a nephew to take the ancient nag to an auction. But upon arriving at the place and finding the beast no longer in the pasture, the nephew, who had never heard of Simpson's trading ways, assumed the horse had been sold by his uncle before he departed on the train.

Simpson fattened the aged animal, keeping him for several weeks, at early morning or after nightfall, in one neighbor's pasture after another, and then he exchanged him with a Milltown man for a top buggy. At this point the Widow Rideout missed her sleigh from where it had rested on the rafters of her carriage house for fifteen years. She had no use for it, and it might have sat unused for another fifteen, but it was her property, and she did not intend to part with it without a struggle. Such is the suspicious nature of the Riverboro Village mind that the moment she discovered her loss she at once thought of Abner Simpson.

So complicated was the nature of this business transaction, because the horse's owner had left the state months earlier, that it took the sheriff many weeks to prove Simpson's guilt. Abner himself claimed his complete innocence, and he told the neighbors how a red-haired man in a tweed suit and wearing an old derby hat had got him out of bed one morning about daylight and offered to swap him a good sleigh for an old cider press he had layin' out in his dooryard. The bargain was struck and he, Abner, paid the red-headed stranger four dollars and seventy-five cents to boot. At this point the mysterious stranger unloaded the sleigh, took the press on his wagon, and vanished up the road, never to be seen or heard from afterward.

"If I could ketch that consarned old thief," exclaimed Simpson self-righteously, "I'd make 'im dance — workin'

off a stolen sleigh on me an' takin' away my good money
an' cider press, to say nothin' o' my character!"

"You'll never ketch 'im, Ab," responded the sheriff.
"He's cut off the same piece o' goods as that there cider
press and that there character and that there four-seventy-
five o' yourn. Nobody ever seen any of 'em but you, and
you'll never see 'em again!"

Mrs. Simpson, who was decidedly Abner's better half,
took in washing and went out to do house cleaning, and
the town helped in the feeding and clothing of her children
when Abner was in jail. George Simpson, a lanky boy of
fourteen, did chores on neighboring farms, and the others—Samuel, Clara Belle, Susan, Elijah, and Elisha—went
to school, when sufficiently clothed and not otherwise
more pleasantly engaged.

There were no secrets in the villages that lay along the
banks of the river. There were many hard-working people
among the inhabitants, but life wore away so quietly and
slowly that there was a good deal of spare time for conversation—under the trees at noon in the hayfield, hanging
over the bridge at nightfall, seated about the stove in the
village store of an evening. These meeting places fur-
nished ample ground for the discussion of current events
as viewed by the men, while choir rehearsals, sewing circles, reading societies, church picnics, and the like gave
opportunity for the expression of the ladies' opinion.

There is not an excess of delicacy or chivalry in the
ordinary country school, and several choice conundrums
and bits of verse dealing with the Simpson affair were
passed among the village scholars, uttered always, be it
said to the students' credit, in undertones and when the
Simpson children were not in the group.

Rebecca Randall was of precisely the same stock as
her schoolmates, and she had the same associates as the

rest of her class, so no one can hardly say why she hated
mean gossip and so habitually held herself aloof from it.

Among the Riverboro girls of her own age was a certain one, excellently named Minnie Smellie, who was anything but a general favorite. She was a ferret-eyed, blond-
haired, spindle-legged little creature whose mind was a
cross between that of a parrot and a sheep. She was suspected of copying answers from the other girls' slates, although she had never been caught in the act. Rebecca and
Emma Jane always knew when she had brought a tart or a
slice of layer cake with her school lunch, because on those
days she forsook the cheerful society of her mates and
sought safe solitude in the woods, returning after a time
with a smirk on her smug little face. After one of these
private luncheons Rebecca had been tempted beyond her
strength, and when Minnie took her seat among them
asked, "Is your headache better, Minnie? Let me wipe off
that strawberry jam over your mouth."

There was no jam there, as a matter of fact, but the
guilty Minnie's handkerchief went to her crimson face in a
flash.

Rebecca confessed to Emma Jane that same afternoon
that she felt ashamed of her prank. "I do hate her ways,"
she exclaimed, "but I'm sorry I let her know I suspected
her, and so to make up, I gave her that little piece of broken coral I keep in my bead purse. You know the one?"

"It don't hardly seem as if she deserved that, and her
so greedy," remarked Emma Jane.

"I know it, but it makes me feel better," said Rebecca
generously. "And besides, I've had it two years, and it's
broken, so it wouldn't ever be any real good, beautiful as
it is to look at."

The coral had partly served its purpose to make up the
hurt, when one afternoon Rebecca, who had stayed after

school for her grammar lesson as usual, was returning
home by way of the shortcut. Far ahead, beyond the pasture bars, she spied the Simpson children just entering the
woods. Seesaw was not with them, so she hastened her
steps in order to have some company on her walk home.
They were speedily lost to view, but when she had almost
overtaken them, she heard in the trees beyond Minnie
Smellie's voice lifted high in song and the sound of a
child's sobbing. Clara Belle, Susan, and the twins were
running along the path, and Minnie was dancing up and
down shrieking:

> "What made the sleigh
>   love Simpson so?"
> The eager children cried;
> "Why Simpson loved the sleigh,
>   you know,"
> The teacher quick replied.

The last glimpse of the fleeing Simpson tribe and the
last flutter of their tattered garments disappeared in the
dim distance. The fall of one small stone thrown by the
valiant Elijah, known around the school as "the fighting
twin," did break the stillness of the woods for a moment,
but it did not come within a hundred yards of Minnie, who
shouted "jail birds" at the top of her lungs and then turned
with an agreeable feeling of excitement, to meet Rebecca,
who stood in the center of the path, her eyes blazing in
indignation.

Minnie's face was not pleasant to see, for a coward
caught at the moment of wrongdoing is not an object of
delight.

"Minnie Smellie, if ever — I — catch — you — singing —
that — to — the Simpsons again — do you know what I'll
do?" spat out Rebecca in a tone of concentrated rage.

"I don't know and I don't care," said Minnie haughtily, though her looks said otherwise.

"I'll take that piece of coral away from you, and I *think* I shall slap you besides!"

"You wouldn't darst," retorted Minnie. "If you do, I'll tell my mother and the teacher, so there!"

"I don't care if you tell your mother, my mother, and all your relations, and the president," said Rebecca, gaining courage as the noble words fell from her lips. "I don't care if you tell the whole town, the whole of York County, the State of Maine, everybody in Boston and — and the nation!" she finished grandiloquently. "Now you run home and remember what I say. If you do it again, and especially if you say 'jail birds,' if I think it's right and my duty, I shall punish you somehow."

The next morning at recess Rebecca observed Minnie telling the tale with variations to Huldah Meserve. "She *threatened* me," whispered Minnie, "but I never believe a word she says."

The latter remark was spoken with the direct intention of being overheard, for Minnie had spasms of bravery when well surrounded by the machinery of law and order.

As Rebecca went back to her seat, she asked Miss Dearborn if she might pass a note to Minnie Smellie and received permission. This was the note:

> Of all the girls that are so mean
> There's none like Minnie Smellie;
> I'll take away the gift I gave
> And pound her into jelly.

> P. S. *Now* do you believe me?

> R. Randall

The effect of this rhyme of warning was entirely convincing, and for days afterward whenever Minnie met the Simpsons even a mile from the brick house, she shuddered and held her tongue.

8

THE COLOR OF ROSES

O n the very Friday after the incident with Minnie Smellie and the Simpsons, there were great goings-on in the little schoolhouse on the hill. Friday afternoon was always the time chosen for skits, songs, and recitations, but it cannot be said that it was a gala day. Most of the children hated speaking pieces, hated the chore of learning them, dreaded the danger of forgetting their lines in public.

Miss Dearborn commonly went home with a headache and never left her bed during the rest of the afternoon or evening. And the occasional mother who attended the exercises sat on a front bench with beads of cold sweat on her forehead, listening to the all-too-familiar halts and stammers. Sometimes a bawling first-grader who had completely forgotten his verse would throw himself into his mother's arms and be carried out into the open air, where he was sometimes kissed and occasionally spanked. But in any case, the failure added an extra dash of gloom and dread to the occasion. The arrival of Rebecca at Riverboro School had somehow injected a new spirit into these previously fearful afternoons. She had taught Elijah and Elisha Simpson so that they recited three verses of something with such comical effect that they delighted themselves, the teacher, and the school, while Susan Simpson had been provided with a humorous poem which induced even Minnie Smellie to laugh aloud. Emma Jane and Rebecca had a skit between them, and the sense of companionship buoyed up Emma Jane and gave her self-reliance.

In fact, Miss Dearborn announced on this particular Friday morning that the exercises promised to be so interesting that she had invited the doctor's wife, the minister's wife, two members of the school board, and a few mothers. Ted Perkins was asked to decorate one of the blackboards and Rebecca the other. Ted, who was the star artist of the school, chose the map of North America. But Rebecca liked to draw things before the eyes of the enchanted pupils, so there grew under her skilled fingers an American flag done in red, white, and blue chalk, every star in its right place, every stripe fluttering in the breeze. Beside this appeared a figure of the Statue of Liberty, like the one newly erected in New York Harbor, copied from the top of the cigar box that held the chalk.

Miss Dearborn was delighted. "I propose we give Rebecca a good hand-clapping for such a beautiful picture — one that the whole school may well be proud of!" she declared.

The scholars clapped heartily, and Dick Carter, leaping to his feet, waved his hand and gave a rousing cheer.

Rebecca's heart leaped for joy, and to her confusion she felt the tears welling in her eyes. She could hardly see the way back to her seat, for in her lonely little life she had never been singled out for applause, never lauded, nor clapped, as in this wonderful, dazzling moment. But enthusiasm gives birth to enthusiasm, and wit and talent kindles wit and talent. Alice Robinson proposed that the school should sing "Three Cheers for the Red, White, and Blue!"

and when they came to the chorus, all point to Rebecca's flag. Dick Carter suggested that Ted Perkins and Rebecca Randall should sign their names to their pictures, so that the visitors would know who drew them. Huldah Meserve asked permission to cover the largest holes in the plastered walls with pine boughs and fill the water pail with wild flowers.

Rebecca's mood was above and beyond all practical details. She sat silent, her heart so full of grateful joy that she could hardly remember the lines of her part in the skit. At recess she bore herself modestly in spite of her great triumph, while in the general atmosphere of goodwill the Smellie-Randall hatchet was buried, and Minnie gathered leafy maple branches and covered the rusty stove with them under Rebecca's direction.

Miss Dearborn dismissed the morning session at quarter to twelve, so that those who lived near enough could go home for a change of dress. Emma Jane and Rebecca ran nearly every step of the way from sheer excitement, stopping only to breathe at the stiles over the fences.

"Will your Aunt Miranda let you wear your best or only your buff calico?" asked Emma Jane.

"I think I'll ask Aunt Jane," Rebecca replied. "Oh, if my pink dress was only finished! When I left this morning, Aunt Jane was making the buttonholes!"

"I'm going to ask my mother to let me wear her garnet ring," said Emma Jane. "It would look perfectly elergant flashing in the sun when I point to the flag. Good-by. Don't wait for me going back. I may get a ride."

Rebecca found the side door locked, but she knew that the key was under the step, and so, of course, did everybody else in Riverboro, for they all did about the same thing with it. She unlocked the door and went into the dining room to find her lunch laid on the table and a note from Aunt Jane saying that they had gone to Wareham with Mrs. Robinson in her buckboard wagon.

"I'll wear it," thought Rebecca. "They're not here to ask, and maybe they wouldn't mind a bit. It's only gingham after all, and it wouldn't be so grand if it wasn't new and hadn't tape trimming on it and wasn't pink."

She unbraided her two pigtails, combed out the waves of her hair, and tied them back with a ribbon. Then she changed her shoes and slipped on the pretty new garment, managing to fasten all but the three middle buttons, which she reserved for Emma Jane. Then her eye fell on her cherished pink parasol, the exact match, and the girls had never seen it. It wasn't quite appropriate for school, but she needn't take it into the room. She would wrap it in a piece of paper, just show it, then carry it coming home.

Once downstairs, Rebecca glanced in the sitting room looking glass and was electrified at the vision. It seemed almost as if beauty of apparel could go no further than that heavenly pink gingham dress! The sparkle of her dark eyes, the glow of her cheeks, the sheen of her falling hair passed unnoticed in the all-conquering charm of the rose-colored garment.

Goodness! It was twenty minutes to one and she would be late. She danced out the side door, pulled a pink rose from a bush at the gate, and covered the half mile between the brick house and the seat of learning in an incredibly short time, meeting Emma Jane, also breathless and resplendent, at the entrance.

"Rebecca Randall!" exclaimed Emma Jane, "you're as handsome as a picture!"

"I?" laughed Rebecca. "Nonsense! It's only the pink gingham."

"You're not good-looking every day, but you're different somehow," insisted Emma Jane. "See my garnet ring.

Mother scrubbed it in soap and water. How on earth did your Aunt Miranda let you put on your bran' new dress?"

"They were both away, and I didn't ask," Rebecca answered anxiously. "Why? Do you think they'd have said no?"

"Miss Miranda always says no, doesn't she?" asked Emma Jane.

"Ye — es. But this afternoon is very special — almost like a Sunday school concert."

"Yes," assented Emma Jane. "It is, of course, with your name on the board, and our pointing to the flag, and our elergant dialogue, and all that."

The afternoon was one succession of solid triumphs for everybody concerned. There were no real failures at all, no tears, no parents ashamed of their children. Miss Dearborn heard many admiring remarks made about her ability and wondered whether they belonged to her or partly, at least, to Rebecca. The girl had no more to do for the audience than several others, but she was somehow in the foreground. As things turned out afterward, at village entertainments in the years to come, Rebecca couldn't be kept in the background; it positively refused to hold her. Her worst enemy could not have called her pushy, however. She sought for no chances of display, she was completely lacking in self-consciousness, and she was always eager to bring others into any fun or entertainment. If wherever the king sat was the head of the table, so in the same way wherever Rebecca stood was the center of the stage. Her clear, high voice soared above all the re҆ in the choruses, and somehow everybody watched her, noticed her gestures, her whole-souled singing, her irrepressible enthusiasm.

Finally the Friday school program was all over, and it seemed to Rebecca as if she should never be cool and calm again, as she loitered on the homeward path. There would be no homework, no lessons to learn tonight, and the vision of helping her aunts pack strawberry preserves on the morrow had no terrors for her; all fear was smothered by the radiance that flooded her soul. There were thick, gathering clouds on the horizon, but she took no notice of them except to be glad that she could raise her parasol in the waning sun. She did not tread the solid ground at all or have the sense of belonging to the common human family until she entered the side yard of the brick house and saw her Aunt Miranda seated in the sitting room window. Then, with a rush, Rebecca came back to earth.

9

WILTED ROSES

There she is, over an hour late. A little more and she'd 'a' been caught in the thundershower, but she'd never look ahead," complained Miranda to Jane, "and added to all her other naughtiness, if she ain't rigged out in that new dress, swingin' her sitting room for all the world as if she was play acting. Now I'm the oldest, Jane, and I intend to have my say. If you don't like it, you can go into the kitchen till it's over."

Miranda rose from her rocker, and her high-button shoes beat a firm tattoo across the maple parlor floor as she marched to meet Rebecca in the hall. "Step right in here, young lady. I want to talk to you. What did you put on that good new dress for on a school day without permission?"

"I had intended to ask you at noontime, but you weren't at home, so I couldn't," began Rebecca.

"You intended no such thing! You put it on because you were left alone, though you knew well enough I wouldn't have let you!"

"If I'd been *certain* you wouldn't have let me, I'd never have worn it," said Rebecca, trying to be truthful. "But I wasn't *certain,* and it was worth risking. I thought perhaps you might, if you knew it was almost a real exhibition at school."

"Exhibition!" snapped Miranda. "You are exhibition enough by yourself, I should say! Were you exhibiting your parasol?"

"The parasol *was* silly," confessed Rebecca, hanging her head, "but it's the only time in my whole life when I had anything to match it, and it looked so beautiful with the pink dress! Emma Jane and I spoke a dialogue about a city girl and a country girl, and it occurred to me just the minute before I left for school how nice it would be for the city girl to carry, and it was. I haven't hurt my dress a mite, Aunt Miranda."

"It's the craftiness and underhandedness of your actions that's the worst," said Miranda coldly. "And look at the other things you've done! It seems as if the devil possessed you! You went up the *front* stairs to your room, but you didn't hide your tracks, for you dropped your handkerchief on the carpet on the way up. You left the screen out of your bedroom window for the flies to come in all over the house. You never cleared your lunch from the table nor washed a dirty dish, and you left the side door unlocked from half past twelve to three o'clock, so't anybody could 'a' come in and stolen what they liked!"

Rebecca sank in her chair as she heard the list of her wrongdoings. How could she have been so careless? The tears began to flow as she attempted to explain things that never could be explained or justified before Aunt Miranda.

"Oh, I'm sorry," Rebecca faltered. "I was trimming the schoolroom, and it got late, and I ran all the way home. It was hard getting into my dress alone — there must be twenty buttons up the back, besides hooks at the waist. And I hadn't time to eat but a mouthful. And just at the last minute, when I honestly — honestly — would have thought about clearing away the dishes and locking up, I looked at the clock and knew I could hardly get back to school in time, and I thought how dreadful it would be to go in late and get my first black mark on a Friday afternoon, and the minister's wife and the doctor's wife and the school committee all there!"

"Don't wail and carry on now. It's no good cryin' over spilt milk," answered Miranda. "An ounce of good behavior is worth a pound of repentance. Instead of tryin' to see how little trouble you can make in a house that ain't your own home, it seems as if you tried to see how much you could put us out. Take that rose out of your dress and let me see the spot it's made on your yoke and the rusty holes where the wet pin went in. I ain't got any patience with your flowers and frizzled-out hair and airs and graces. You're for all the world like your no-good, Miss-Nancy father!"

Rebecca lifted her head in a flash. "Look here, Aunt Miranda, I'll be as good as I know how to be. I'll mind quick when I'm spoken to and never leave the door unlocked again, but I won't have my dead father called names. He was a p-perfectly l-lovely father, that's what he was, and it's *mean* of you to call him a 'Miss Nancy!'"

"Don't you dare answer me back that impertinent way, Rebecca, tellin' me I'm mean. Your father was a foolish, shiftless man, an' you might as well hear it from me as from anybody else. He spent your mother's money on empty business ventures and left her with seven children to provide for."

"It's s-something to leave s-seven nice children," sobbed Rebecca.

"Not when other folks have to help feed, clothe, and educate 'em," responded Miranda. "Now you step upstairs, put on your nightgown, go to bed, and stay there till morn-

*"You're for all the world like your no-good,
Miss-Nancy father!"*

ing. You'll find a bowl of crackers and milk on your bureau, an' I don't want to hear a sound from you till breakfast time. Jane, run and take the dish towels off the clothesline and shut the woodshed doors. We're goin' to have a terrible shower."

"We've had it, I should think," murmured Jane as she went to do her sister's bidding. "I don't often speak my mind, Miranda, but you ought not to have said what you did about Lorenzo Randall. He was what he was, and things can't be made any different, but he was Rebecca's father, and Aurelia always says he was a good husband."

"Yes, I've noticed that dead husbands are usually good ones," Miranda answered grimly. "But the truth needs an airin' now an' then, and that child will never amount to a hill of beans till she gets some of her father trounced out of her. I'm glad I said just what I did."

"I daresay you are," remarked Jane, with one of her annual bursts of courage. "But all the same, Miranda, it wasn't good manners, and it wasn't good Christianity!"

The clap of thunder that shook the house just at that moment made no such peal in Miranda Sawyer's ears as Jane's remark did when it fell with a deafening roar on her conscience. Though Miranda had for many years buried all feelings of kindness toward children, God was at work in her heart.

Perhaps, after all, it is just as well to speak up only once a year, and then speak to the purpose.

Rebecca mounted the back stairs wearily, the creaking of the worn, old steps matching the groaning in her heart. She closed the door to her bedroom and took off the beloved pink gingham dress with trembling fingers. Her cotton handkerchief was rolled into a hard ball, and between reaching for the more difficult buttons that lay between her shoulder blades and her belt, she dabbed her wet eyes carefully, so that they should not rain salt water on the finery that had been worn at such a painful price. She smoothed it out carefully, pinched up the white ruffle at the neck, stretched the dress over a wooden hanger, and hung it in her closet with an extra little sob at the roughness of life.

The withered pink rose fell on the floor. Rebecca stared at it and thought, *Just like my happy day.* Nothing could show more clearly the kind of child she was than that she instantly perceived the symbolism of the rose and laid it away on a closet shelf next to the dress as if she were burying the whole episode with all its sad memories. It was a child's poetic instinct with a dawning hint of a woman's sentiment in it.

She braided her hair in the two accustomed pigtails, took off her best shoes, which had happily escaped Aunt Miranda's notice, with all the while a fixed resolve growing in her mind, that of leaving the brick house and going back to the farm. She knew she would not be received there with open arms, but she would help her mother about the house and send her sister Hannah to Riverboro in her place.

She sat by the window trying to make some sort of plan, watching the lightning play over the hilltop and the streams of rain chasing each other down the lightning rod. And this was the day that had dawned so joyfully! It had been a red sunrise, and she had leaned on the windowsill studying her lesson and thinking what a lovely world it was. And what a golden morning it had been! The changing of the bare, ugly little schoolroom into a bower of beauty; Miss Dearborn's pleasure at her success with the Simpson twins' recitation; the privilege of decorating the blackboard; the happy thought of drawing the Statue of Liberty from the picture on a cigar box; the intoxicating moment when the school clapped for her! And what an afternoon! How it had gone on from glory to glory, beginning with Emma Jane's telling her, Rebecca Randall, that she was as "handsome as a picture!"

Rebecca lived through the school exercises again in her memory, especially her dialogue with Emma Jane and her inspiration of using the bough-covered stove as a mossy bank where the country girl could sit and watch her sheep. This had given Emma Jane a feeling of such ease that she never recited her lines better. And how generous it was of her to lend her garnet ring to the city girl, imagining the awestruck shepherd girl!

Rebecca had thought Aunt Miranda might be pleased that the niece invited down from the farm had succeeded so well at school. But no, there was no hope of pleasing her in that or in any other way. She would go to Maplewood on the stage next day with Mr. Cobb and get home somehow from Cousin Ann's.

On second thought, she realized her aunts might not allow it. Very well, she would slip away now and see if she could stay all night with the Cobbs and be off next morning before breakfast. Rebecca put on her oldest dress and hat and jacket, then wrapped her nightgown, comb, and toothbrush in a bundle and dropped it softly out the window. Her room was in the low wing of the house, and her window was not at a very dangerous distance from the ground, though even had it been high up, nothing could have stopped her at that moment.

Somebody who had climbed on the roof to clean out the gutters had left a cleat nailed to the side of the house about halfway between the window and the roof of the back porch. Rebecca heard the sound of the treadle sewing machine in the dining room and the chopping of meat in the kitchen, so knowing where both her aunts were, she scrambled out the window, caught hold of the lightning

She scrambled out the window, caught hold of the
lightning rod ground cable . . .

rod ground cable, slid down to the helpful cleat, jumped to the porch roof, then used the woodbine trellis for a ladder to the ground. She was flying up the road before she had time to consider the consequences of running away.

Jeremiah Cobb sat at supper at the table by the kitchen window. "Mother," as he was in the habit of calling his wife, was away nursing a sick neighbor. Mrs. Cobb was mother only to a little gravestone in the church cemetery, where reposed "Sarah Ann, beloved daughter of Jeremiah and Sarah Cobb, aged 17 months."

The thunder and lightning were done, but the rain still fell and the heavens were dark, though it was scarcely five o'clock. Looking up from his cup of tea, the old man saw at the open door a very picture of woe. Rebecca's face was so swollen with tears and misery that for a moment Mr. Cobb scarcely recognized her. Then, when he heard her voice asking, "Please may I come in, Mr. Cobb?" he jumped to his feet.

"Well, I vow!" he cried. "It's my little lady passenger! Come to call on old Uncle Jerry and pass the evening, have ye? Why, you're wet as sops. Draw up to the stove. I made a fire thinkin' I wanted something warm for supper, being kind of lonesome here without Mother. She's settin' up with sick Seth Strout tonight. There, we'll hang your soppy hat on a hook, put your jacket over the drying rod behind the stove, and then you turn your back to the stove and dry yourself good."

Uncle Jerry had never before said so many words at a time, but he had caught sight of the child's red eyes and tear-stained cheeks, and his big heart went out to her trouble, quite regardless of any circumstances that might have caused it.

Rebecca stood still for a moment until Uncle Jerry took his seat again at the table, and then, unable to contain herself any longer, she cried, "Oh, Mr. Cobb, I've run away from the brick house, and I want to go back to the farm. Will you keep me here tonight and take me up to Maplewood in the stagecoach tomorrow? I haven't got any money for my fare, but I'll earn it somehow afterward."

"Well, I guess we won't quarrel about the money, you and me," said the old man. "We've never had our ride together, anyway, though we always meant to go down river, not up."

"I shall never see Milltown now," sobbed Rebecca.

"Come over here 'side of me and tell me all about it," coaxed Uncle Jerry. "Just set down on that there wooden stool an' out with the whole story."

Rebecca leaned her aching head against Mr. Cobb's kindly knee and repeated the history of her trouble with Aunt Miranda. Tragic as that history seemed to her passionate and undisciplined mind, she told it truthfully and without exaggeration.

10

RAINBOW BRIDGES

U ncle Jerry coughed and stirred in his chair a good deal as Rebecca told her sad story, but he carefully concealed any undue feeling of sympathy, just muttering, "Poor little soul! We'll see what we can do for you!"

"You will take me to Maplewood, won't you, Mr. Cobb?" begged Rebecca piteously.

"Don't you fret a mite," he answered, the Lord guiding him as he listened to her troubles. "I'll see you through somehow. Now take a bite o' something to eat, child. Spread some of that strawberry preserve on your bread. Draw up to the table. How'd you like to sit in Mother's place an' pour me another cup of hot tea?"

Uncle Jerry Cobb's mental machinery was simple, but it moved smoothly when propelled by his affection and sympathy. So praying for some flash of inspiration to light his path, he felt his way along, trusting God to direct him.

Rebecca, comforted by the old man's tone, and timidly enjoying the dignity of sitting in Mrs. Cobb's seat and lifting the blue china teapot, smiled faintly, smoothed her hair, and dried her eyes.

"I suppose your mother'll be terrible glad to see you back again?" queried Mr. Cobb.

A tiny fear—just a baby thing in the bottom of Rebecca's heart—stirred and grew larger the moment it was touched with this question.

"She won't like it that I ran away, I suppose, and she'll be sorry that I couldn't please Aunt Miranda. But I'll make her understand, just as I did you."

"I s'pose she was thinking of your schoolin', lettin' you come down here. But land, you can go to school in Temperance, I s'pose?"

"There's only two months of school now in Temperance, and Sunnybrook Farm's too far from all the other schools."

"Oh, well, there's other things in the world besides education," responded Uncle Jerry, cutting himself a piece of apple pie. He held the pie up for Rebecca, but she shook her head vigorously.

"Ye-es, though Mother thought education was going to be the making of me," returned Rebecca sadly, giving a dry little sob as she tried to drink her tea.

"It'll be nice for you to be all together again at the farm—such a house full o' children!" remarked the dear old gentleman, who longed for nothing so much as to cuddle and comfort the poor little creature.

"It's too full—that's the trouble. But I'll make sister Hannah come to Riverboro in my place."

"S'pose Miranda 'n' Jane'll have her? I should be 'most afraid they wouldn't. They'll be kind o' mad at your goin' home, you know, and you can hardly blame 'em."

This was quite a new thought—that the brick house might be closed to Hannah since she, Rebecca, had turned her back upon its hospitality.

"How is this school down here in Riverboro—pretty good?" inquired Uncle Jerry.

"Oh, it's a splendid school! And Miss Dearborn is a splendid teacher!"

"You like her, do you? Well, you'd better believe she returns the compliment. Mother was down to Watson's store this afternoon buying liniment for sick Seth Strout, and she met Miss Dearborn on the bridge. They got to talkin' 'bout school, for Mother had boarded a lot of the school marms and likes 'em. 'How does the little Temperance girl get along?' asks Mother. 'Oh, she's the best scholar I have!' says Miss Dearborn. 'I could teach school from sunup to sundown if my students were all like Rebecca Randall,' says she."

"Oh, Uncle Jerry Cobb, *did* she say that?" glowed Rebecca, her face sparkling and dimpling in an instant. "I've tried hard all the time, but I'll study the covers right off the books now."

"You mean you would if you'd been goin' to stay here," interposed Uncle Jerry. "Now ain't it too bad you've just got to give it all up on account of Aunt Miranda? Well, I can hardly blame ye. She can be cranky and sour. But you need to bear with her, and I guess you ain't much on patience, be ye?"

"Not very much," admitted Rebecca dolefully.

"If I'd had this talk with ye yesterday," pursued Mr. Cobb, "I believe I'd have advised ye different. It's too late now, and I don't feel to say you've been all in the wrong. But if it was to do over again, I'd say, well, your Aunt Miranda gives you clothes and board and schooling and is goin' to send you to Wareham Academy at a big expense. She kind of heaves her benefits at your head, same's she would bricks, but they're benefits, just the same. And mebbe it's your job to kind of pay for them in good behavior. Jane's a leetle bit more easygoin' than Miranda, ain't she? Or is she just as hard to please?"

"Oh, Aunt Jane and I get along splendidly," exclaimed Rebecca. "She's just as good and kind as she can be, and I like her better all the time. I think she kind of likes me, too; she smoothed my hair once. I'd let her scold me all day long, for she understands, but she can't stand up for me against Aunt Miranda. She's about afraid of her as I am."

"Jane'll be real sorry tomorrow to find you've gone away, I guess. But never mind. It can't be helped. If she has kind of a dull time with Miranda, why, of course she'd set great store by your company. Mother was talkin' with her at church after prayer meeting the other night. 'You wouldn't know the brick house, Sarah,' says Jane. 'I'm keeping a sewing school, and my pupil has made herself three dresses. What do you think of that,' says she, 'for an old maid's child? I've started teaching a class in Sunday school,' says Jane, 'and I'm thinking of renewin' my youth and goin' to the church picnic with Rebecca,' says she. And Mother declares she never saw her look so young an' happy."

"I do *so* wish that Aunt Miranda'd be more understanding, like Aunt Jane," responded Rebecca. "She never misses church or prayer meeting 'less she's sick. Why, she's more regular than Aunt Jane! Why are people so different, Uncle Jerry?"

Jeremiah Cobb pushed a hand through his thin gray hair and leaned back in his chair. "Seems as if church doesn't have the same effect on everybody. Like it says in the Bible, some folks begin in the spirit but try to continue in the flesh. They try to become better Christians in their own strength, rather'n let the Lord work in their hearts. I think your Aunt Miranda'll come around, but it may take a while yet," Uncle Jerry remarked, displaying unusual insight for an unlettered old man.

There was silence that could be felt in the little kitchen, a silence broken only by the ticking of the old mantle clock and the beating of Rebecca's heart, which, it seemed to her, almost drowned the voice of the clock.

"Uncle Jerry," she said to the old man quietly, "sometimes in church I try to pray, but my prayers seem to get only to the ceiling. I'd like to go back to the brick house and live with Aunt Jane — really I would. But I've so much anger inside me — God won't hear my prayers for Aunt Jane when my heart is so full of anger toward Aunt Miranda, will He?" she said at last.

"Rebecca, Jesus is able to make us love ev'n our enemies — not to speak of an aunt. First, you've got to let Jesus be yer friend. You already know that Jesus died for you. And ye know that you can't be good by yourself; you need to know how to get Jesus' goodness fer yourself. You can't work an' earn it. You need to ask Him for help 'n' to be yer Savior."

"All right, Uncle Jerry, I will." And Rebecca bowed her head and prayed, "Dear God — dear Jesus, I've tried to be good, but I know that I can't be good enough by myself. Forgive me for hating Aunt Miranda. Please help me and save me from my sins."

The rain ceased, a sudden rosy light filled the room, and through the window a rainbow arch could be seen spanning the heavens like a radiant bridge. *Bridges one took across difficult places,* thought Rebecca, and Uncle Jerry seemed to have built one over her troubles, and the Lord had given her strength to walk across. Rebecca had crossed over to a new life in Jesus.

"The shower's over," said the old man, pouring himself another cup of tea. "It's cleared the air, washed the face o' the earth nice an' clean, an' everything tomorrow will shine like a new pin — when you and I are driving up river in the coach."

Rebecca pushed her cup away, rose from the table, and put on her hat and jacket quietly. "I'm not going up river with you, Uncle Jerry," she said. "I'm going to stay here and — and catch bricks, catch 'em without throwing 'em back, too. I don't know as Aunt Miranda will take me in after I've run away, but I'm going back now while I have the courage. You wouldn't be so good as to go with me, would you, Uncle Jerry?"

"You'd better believe your Uncle Jerry don't propose to leave till he gets this thing fixed up," cried the old man delightedly. "Now you've had all you can stand tonight, poor little soul, without getting a fit of sickness, an' Miranda'll be sore an' cross and in no condition for argument, so my plan is just this: to drive you over to the brick house in my top buggy; to have you sit back in the corner, and I get out and go to the side door. And when I get your Aunt Miranda 'n' Aunt Jane out into the shed to plan where to stack a load of firewood I'm going to haul for them later this week, you'll slip out of the buggy and go upstairs to bed. The front door won't be locked, will it?"

"Not this time of night," Rebecca answered. "Not till Aunt Miranda goes to bed. But oh, what if it should be?"

"Well it won't, and if 'tis, why we'll have to face it, though in my opinion there's things that won't bear facin' and had better be settled comfortable an' quiet. You see, you ain't run away yet. You've only come over here to consult me about runnin' away, and we've concluded it ain't worth the trouble. The only thing you've done wrong, as I figger it out, was in coming over here by the window when you'd been sent to bed. You can tell Aunt Jane about it come Sunday after church. Now come on. I'm all hitched up to go over to the post office. Don't forget your bundle—'it's always a journey, Mother, when you carry a nightgown.' Them's the first words your Uncle Jerry ever heard you say," he slyly remarked. "I didn't think you'd be bringing your nightgown over to my house. Step in and curl up in the corner of the buggy seat. We ain't going to let folks see a little runaway girl, 'cause she's going to begin all over again."

&a &a &a

Rebecca crept upstairs, and undressing in the dark, slipped into her nightgown and crawled back into her own bed. Though she was aching and throbbing in every nerve, she felt a new kind of peace stealing over her. She had been saved from foolishness and error by the godly advice of dear old Uncle Jerry, and this had kept her from troubling her poor mother and prevented her from angering and mortifying her aunts.

Her heart was melted now, and Rebecca was determined to win Aunt Miranda's approval by showing her Jesus' love. She was determined also to try to forget the one thing that upset her the most—Aunt Miranda's scornful mention of her father for whom she had the greatest admiration and whom she had not yet heard criticized, for the sorrows and disappointments that Aurelia Randall had suffered she had never communicated to her children.

It would have been some comfort to the bruised little spirit to know that Miranda Sawyer was passing an uncomfortable night and that she regretted her harshness, partly because Jane had taken such a lofty and virtuous position in the matter. Miranda could not endure Jane's disapproval, although she would never have admitted such a weakness.

As Uncle Jerry drove his buggy homeward under the stars, well content with his attempts at keeping the peace, he thought wistfully of the touch of Rebecca's head on his

knee and the rain of her tears on his hand. He thought of
the sweet reasonableness of her mind when she had had
the matter put rightly before her and of the touching hun-
ger for love and understanding that were so characteristic
of her. "To hector an' abuse a child like that one," he said
under his breath. "'Twouldn't be abuse to some of your
elephant-hided young-uns. But to that tender little will-o'-
the-wisp, a hard word's like a lash. Miranda Sawyer would
be a heap better woman if she had a little gravestone to
remember, same's Mother and I have."

ðə   ðə   ðə

"I never saw a child improve in her work as Rebecca
has today," remarked Miranda Sawyer to Jane on Saturday
evening. "That scolding I gave her was probably just what
she needed, and I daresay it'll last for a month."

"I'm glad you're pleased," answered Jane. "A cringing
worm is what you want, not a bright, smiling child. If you
follow my advice, which you seldom do, you'll let me
take her and Emma Jane down beside the river tomorrow
after church, and bring Emma Jane home to a good Sunday supper. Then, if you'll let her go to Milltown with the
Cobbs on Wednesday, that'll hearten her up a little.
Wednesday's a school holiday because Miss Dearborn's
going home to her sister's wedding, and the Cobbs and
Perkinses want to go down to the York County Agricul-
tural Fair."

11

WIDENING HORIZONS

Rebecca's visit to Milltown was all that her glowing fancy had painted it, except that her recent readings about Rome and Venice caused her to believe that those cities might be even more beautiful than Milltown. So soon does the soul outgrow its mansions that after she had once seen Milltown, her imagination ran out to the future sight of Portland. That city, having islands and a harbor and two public monuments, she felt, must be far more beautiful than Milltown.

It would be impossible for two children to see more, do more, walk more, talk more, eat more, or ask more questions than Rebecca and Emma Jane did on that eventful Wednesday in Milltown.

"She's the best company I ever saw in all my life," said Mrs. Cobb to her husband that evening. "We haven't had a dull minute this day. She's well mannered, too. She didn't ask for anything and was thankful for whatever she got. Did you watch her face when we went into that tent where they were actin' *Uncle Tom's Cabin!* And did you take notice of the way she told us about how she had read the book when we sat down to have our ice cream? I tell

you Harriet Beecher Stowe herself couldn't have done it
better justice!"

"I took it all in," responded Mr. Cobb, who was
pleased that Mother agreed with him about Rebecca. "I
ain't sure, but she's goin' to turn out somethin' remarkable — a singer, or a writer, or a lady doctor like that Miss
Parks up to Cornish."

"I can't see Rebecca as a lady doctor somehow,"
mused Mrs. Cobb. "Her gift of gab is what's going to be
the makin' of her. Maybe she'll lecture or recite poetry,
like that Portland poet, Henry Longfellow, that come out
here to the harvest supper."

"I guess she'll be able to write down her own poems,"
said Mr. Cobb confidently. "She could make 'em up
faster'n she could read 'em out of a book."

"It's a pity she's so plain looking," remarked Mrs.
Cobb, blowing out the lamp.

"Plain looking, Mother?" exclaimed her husband in astonishment. "Look at the eyes of her! Look at the hair of
her, an' the smile, an' that there dimple! I hope Miranda'll
favor her comin' over to see us real often, for she'll let off
some of her steam here, an' the brick house'll be considerable happier for everybody concerned. We've known what
it was to have children, even if it was more'n thirty years
ago, and we can make allowances."

≈a   ≈a   ≈a

Notwithstanding the praises of Mr. and Mrs. Cobb,
Rebecca's composition writing was still very immature at
this time. Miss Dearborn gave her every sort of subject
that she had ever been given herself: "Cloud Pictures,"
"Abraham Lincoln," "Nature," "Philanthropy," "Slavery,"
"The Example of Christ," "Joy and Duty," "Solitude." But
Rebecca, as much as she enjoyed writing, couldn't seem to
fully satisfy Miss Dearborn with any of her efforts.

"Write as you talk, Rebecca," insisted Miss Dearborn one day, though she secretly knew that she herself could never manage a good composition.

"But gracious me, Miss Dearborn! I don't talk about nature and slavery. I can't write unless I have something to say, can I?"

"That is what compositions are for," returned Miss Dearborn doubtfully, "to make you have things to say. Now in your last one, on solitude, you haven't said anything very interesting, and you've made it too common and everyday to sound well. There are too many 'yous' and 'yours' in it. You ought to say 'one' now and then, to make it seem more like good writing. 'One opens a favorite book,' 'One's thoughts are a great comfort in solitude,' and so on."

"I don't know any more about solitude this week than I did about joy and duty last week," grumbled Rebecca.

"You tried to be funny about joy and duty," said Miss Dearborn reprovingly, "so, of course, you didn't succeed."

"I didn't know you were going to make us read the things out loud," said Rebecca with an embarrassed smile of recollection.

"Joy and Duty" had been the inspiring subject given to the older children for a theme to be written in five minutes. Rebecca had wrestled, struggled, perspired in vain. When her turn came to read, she said she had written nothing.

"You have at least two lines, Rebecca," insisted the teacher, "for I see them on your slate."

"I'd rather not read them, please. They are no good," pleaded Rebecca.

"Read what you have, good or bad. I am excusing nobody."

Rebecca rose, overcome with secret laughter, dread, and mortification. Then in a low voice she read her couplet:

> When Joy and Duty clash
> Let Duty go to smash.

Dick Carter's head disappeared under the desk, while Ted Perkins choked with laughter. Miss Dearborn laughed, too. She was still a teen herself, and the idea of making dour adults of children seldom appealed to her sense of humor.

"You must stay after school and try again, Rebecca," she said, but she said it smilingly. "Your poetry hasn't a very nice idea in it for a good little girl who ought to love duty."

"It wasn't my idea," said Rebecca apologetically. "I had only written the first line when I saw you were going to ring the bell and say the time was up. I had 'clash' written, and I couldn't think of anything then but 'hash' or 'rash' or 'smash.' I'll change it to this:

> When Joy and Duty clash,
> 'Tis Joy must go to smash."

"That is better," Miss Dearborn agreed, "though I cannot think 'going to smash' is a pretty expression for poetry."

Since Miss Dearborn had instructed her in the use of the indefinite pronoun *one* as giving a refined and elegant touch to her writing, Rebecca painstakingly rewrote her composition on solitude. It then appeared in the following form, which hardly satisfied either teacher or pupil.

Solitude

It would be false to say that one could ever be alone when one has one's lovely thoughts to comfort one. One sits by one's self, it is true, but one thinks. One opens one's favorite book and reads one's favorite story. One speaks to one's aunt or one's brother, pats one's cat, or looks at one's photograph album.

There is one's work also. What a joy it is to one, if one happens to like work. All one's little household tasks keep one from being lonely. Does one ever feel lonely when one picks up one's chips of kindling wood to light one's fire for one's evening meal? Or when one washes one's milk pail before milking one's cow? One would fancy not.

"It is perfectly dreadful," sighed Rebecca when she read it aloud after school. "Putting in *one* all the time doesn't make it sound any more like a book, and it looks silly besides."

"You say such queer things," objected Miss Dearborn. "I don't see what makes you do it. Why did you put in anything so common as picking up chips?"

"Because I was talking about 'household tasks' in the sentence before, and it *is* one of my household tasks. And don't you think calling supper 'one's evening meal' is pretty?"

"Yes, that part of it does sound very well. It is the cat, the chips, and the milk pail that I don't like."

"All right," sighed Rebecca. "Out they go! Does the cow go too?"

"Yes. I don't like a cow in a composition," said the difficult Miss Dearborn, who was struggling with learning to write well herself.

᠔ ᠔ ᠔

The Milltown trip created its own troubles for Rebecca, for the next week Minnie Smellie's mother told Miranda Sawyer that she'd better look after Rebecca, for she had been using "swear words and profane language," and that she had been heard saying something dreadful that very afternoon, saying it before Emma Jane and Ted Perkins, who only laughed and got down on all fours and chased her.

Rebecca, on being confronted with the crime, denied it indignantly, and Aunt Jane believed her.

"Search your memory, Rebecca, and try to think what Minnie overheard you say," Aunt Jane pleaded, hoping to spare Rebecca Aunt Miranda's wrath. "Think real hard. When did they chase you up the road, and what were you doing?"

A sudden light broke upon Rebecca's darkness. "Oh, I see it now," she exclaimed. "It had rained hard all the morning, you know, and the road was full of puddles. Ted and I were walking along, and I was ahead. I saw the water streaming over the road towards the ditch, and it reminded me of the *Uncle Tom's Cabin* play in a tent at Milltown, when Eliza took her baby and ran across the Mississippi on the ice blocks, pursued by the bloodhounds. We couldn't keep from laughing after we came out of the tent because they were acting on such a small platform that Eliza had to run 'round an' 'round, and part of the time one dog chased her, and part of the time she had to chase the dog. I knew Ted would remember, too, so I took off my raincoat and wrapped it 'round my books for a baby. Then I shouted, *'My God! The river!'* just like that — the same as Eliza did in the play. Then I leaped from puddle to puddle, and Ted and Em chased me like bloodhounds. It's just like that stupid Minnie Smellie who doesn't know a game when she sees one. And Eliza wasn't swearing when she said, 'My God! The river!' It was more like praying."

"Well, you've got no reason to be prayin', any more than swearin' in the middle of the road," said Miranda, "but I'm thankful it's no worse. You're born to trouble as the sparks that fly upward, an' I'm afraid you always will be till you learn to bridle your unruly tongue."

"I wish sometimes that I could bridle Minnie's tongue," murmured Rebecca under her breath as she went to set the table for supper. Though angry, she was thankful to have got off with only a scolding.

"I declare she is the beatin'est child!" said Miranda, taking off her spectacles and laying down her mending. "You don't think she's a little mite crazy, do you, Jane?"

"I don't think she's like the rest of us," responded Jane thoughtfully, but with some anxiety in her pleasant face. "But whether it's for the better or the worse I can't tell till she grows up an' we kin see what the Lord intends her to become. She's got the makin' of 'most anything in her, Rebecca has, but I feel sometimes as if we were not fitted to cope with her."

"Stuff an' nonsense!" said Miranda. "Speak for yourself. I feel fitted to cope with any child that ever was born in the world!"

"I know you do, Miranda, but that don't *make* it so," returned Jane with a smile.

The habit of speaking her mind freely was certainly growing on Jane to an altogether terrifying extent.

12

RED PAINT AND PINK GINGHAM

C lad in her best dress, Rebecca went one day to take tea with the Cobbs, but while crossing the bridge, she was suddenly overcome by the beauty of the river and leaned over the newly painted rail to feast her eyes on the dashing torrent of the waterfalls. Resting her elbows on the topmost board and inclining her little figure forward in delicious ease, she stood there dreaming.

The river above the dam was a glassy lake with all the loveliness of the blue heaven and green shore reflected in its surface. The falls was a whirling wonder of water, ever pouring itself over and over, inexhaustible in luminous golden gushes that lost themselves in snowy depths of foam. The river above the dam lay cold and gray beneath the leaden November sky, but swollen with turbulent power as it plummeted over the dam and beneath the bridge. How many young eyes had gazed into the mystery and majesty of the several falls along the Saco River, and how many young hearts dreamed about their futures leaning over that very bridge rail, seeing the vision reflected

*. . . inclining her little figure forward in delicious
ease, she stood there dreaming.*

there and often, too, watching it fade into the light of common day?

Rebecca never went across the bridge without bending over the rail to wonder and to ponder, and at this special moment she was putting the finishing touches on a poem:

> Two maidens by a river strayed
> Down in the state of Maine.
> The one was called Rebecca,
> The other Emma Jane.
>
> "I wish my life were like the stream,"
> Said her named Emma Jane,
> "So quiet and so very smooth,
> So free from every pain."
>
> "I'd rather be a little drop
> In the great rushing fall!
> I would not choose the glassy lake,
> 'Twould not suit me at all!"
> (It was the dark-haired maiden spoke
> The words I just have stated,
> The maidens two were simply friends
> And not at all related.)
>
> But O! Alas! We may not have
> The things we hope to gain;
> The quiet life may come to me,
> The rush to Emma Jane!

"I don't like 'the rush to Emma Jane,' and I can't think of anything else. Oh, what a smell of turpentine! Oh, the paint is *on* me! Oh, it's all over my best dress! Oh, what *will* Aunt Miranda say!"

With tears of self-reproach streaming from her eyes, Rebecca flew up the hill, sure of sympathy and hoping against hope for help of some sort.

Mrs. Cobb took in the situation at a glance and professed herself able to remove almost any stain from almost any fabric, and Uncle Jerry agreed with her, vowing, "Mother can git anything out. Sometimes she takes the cloth right along with the spot, but she has a sure hand, Mother has!"

The damaged garment was removed and partially immersed in turpentine, while Rebecca sat at the table clad in a blue calico robe of Mrs. Cobb's.

"Don't let it take your appetite away," crooned Mrs. Cobb. "I've got cream biscuit and honey for you. If the turpentine don't work, I'll try French chalk, magnesia, and warm suds. If they fail, Father shall run over to Strout's and borry some of the stuff Martha got in Milltown to take the currant pie out of her weddin' dress."

"I ain't got to understandin' this paintin' accident yet," said Uncle Jerry jocosely as he handed Rebecca the honey. "Bein' as how there's 'Fresh Paint' signs hung all over the bridge, so't a blind person couldn't miss 'em, I can't hardly account for your gettin' into the pesky stuff."

"I didn't notice the signs," Rebecca said dolefully. "I suppose I was looking at the falls."

"The falls has been there since Noah's Flood, an' I calculate they'll be there till the end of time, so you needn't 'a' been in sich a brash rush to git a sight of 'em. Children comes terrible high, Mother, but I s'pose we must have 'em!" he said, winking at Mrs. Cobb.

When supper was cleared away, Rebecca insisted on washing and wiping the dishes, while Mrs. Cobb worked on the dress with an energy that plainly showed the seriousness of the task. Rebecca kept leaving her job at the sink to bend anxiously over the basin and watch her progress, while Uncle Jerry offered advice from time to time.

"You musta' laid all over the bridge, deary," said Mrs. Cobb, "for the paint's not only on your elbows and yoke and waist, but it about covers your front breadth."

As the garment began to look a little better, Rebecca's spirits took an upward turn, and at length she left it to dry in the fresh evening air and went into the sitting room.

"Have you a piece of paper please?" asked Rebecca. "I'll write down the poetry I was making while I was lying in the paint."

Mrs. Cobb sat by her mending basket, and Uncle Jerry took down a gingham bag of strings and occupied himself in taking the snarls out of them — a favorite evening amusement with him.

Rebecca soon had the lines written out in her round schoolgirl hand, making such improvements as occurred to her on sober second thought.

The Two Wishes
by
Rebecca Randall

Two maidens by a river strayed,
'Twas in the state of Maine.
Rebecca was the darker one,
The fairer, Emma Jane.

The fairer maiden said, "I wish
My life were as the stream,
So peaceful, and so smooth and still,
So pleasant and serene."

"I'd rather be a little drop
In the great rushing fall;
I'd never choose the quiet lake;
'Twould not please me at all."

(It was the dark-haired maiden spoke
The words we just have stated;
The maidens twain were simply friends,
Not sisters nor related.)

But O! Alas! we may not have
The things we hope to gain.
The quiet life may come to me,
The rush to Emma Jane!

Rebecca read it aloud, and the Cobbs thought it a sur-passingly beautiful and marvelous poem.

"I guess if that writer that lived on Congress Street in Portland could 'a' heard your poetry, he'd 'a' been astonished," said Mrs. Cobb. "If you ask me, I say this piece is as good as that one o' his, 'Tell me not, in mournful numbers,' and consid'ably clearer."

"I never could fairly figger out what 'mournful numbers' was," remarked Mr. Cobb critically.

"Then I guess you never studied fractions!" joked Rebecca. "See here, Uncle Jerry and Aunt Sarah, do you think I should write another verse, especially for a last one, as they usually do—one with 'thoughts' in it—to make a better ending?"

"If you can grind 'em out just by turnin' the crank, why I should say the more the merrier, but I don't hardly see how you could have a better endin'," observed Mr. Cobb.

"It is *horrid!*" grumbled Rebecca. "I ought not to have put that 'me' in. I'm writing the poetry. Nobody ought to know it *is* me standing by the river. It ought to be 'Rebecca' or 'the dark-haired maiden,' and 'the rush to Emma Jane' is simply dreadful. Sometimes I think I never will try poetry; it's so hard to make it come out right, and other times it just says itself. I wonder if this would be better:

> But Oh, alas! we may not gain
> The good which we desire;
> The quiet life may come to one
> Who likes his life afire.

"I don't know if that is worse or not. Now for a new last verse!" In a few minutes the poetess looked up, happy and triumphant. "It was easy as nothing. Just hear!" And she read slowly, with her pretty, musical voice:

> Then if our lot be bright or sad,
> Be full of smiles or tears,
> The thought that God has planned it so
> Should help us bear the years.

Mr. and Mrs. Cobb exchanged speechless glances of admiration. Indeed, Uncle Jerry was obliged to turn his face to the window and wipe his tears furtively with his big handkerchief.

"How in the world did ye do it?" Mrs. Cobb exclaimed.

"Oh, it's easy," answered Rebecca. "The hymns at church are all like that. You see, there's a school newspaper printed at Wareham Academy once a month. Dick Carter says the editor is always a boy, of course, but he allows the girls to try and write for it and then chooses the best. Dick thinks I can be in it."

"*In* it!" exclaimed Uncle Jerry. "I shouldn't be a bit surprised if they had you write the whole paper, an' as for any boy editor, you could lick him writin', I bet ye, with one hand tied behind ye, and yer best hand at that!"

"Can we have a copy of your poetry to keep in our family Bible?" inquired Mrs. Cobb respectfully.

"Oh, would you like it?" asked Rebecca. "Yes, indeed! I'll do a clean, nice one with violet ink and a fine quill pen. But I must go and look at my poor dress."

They followed Rebecca into the kitchen. The dress was quite dry, and in truth it had been helped a little by Aunt Sarah's scrubbing it in turpentine. But the colors had run in the rubbing, the pattern was blurred, and there were muddy streaks here and there. As a last resort, it was carefully smoothed with a warm iron, and Rebecca was urged to dress herself, so they might see if the spots showed as much when it was on.

They did show most uncompromisingly and even to the dullest eye. Rebecca gave one searching look in the mirror and then said, as she took her hat from a nail in the entry, "I think I'll be going. Good night. If I've got to have a scolding, I want it quick, and get it over with."

"Poor little unlucky, misfortunate thing," sighed Uncle Jerry as his eyes followed her down the hill. "I wish she could pay some attention to the ground under her feet, but I vow, if she were ourn, I'd let her slop paint all over the house before I could scold her. Here's her poetry she's left behind. Listen as I read it aloud again, Mother. Land," he continued, chuckling, "I can just see the last flap o' that boy editor's shirttails as he legs it for the woods while Becky settles down in his revolvin' chair! I'm puzzled as to what kind of a job editin' is, exactly, but she'll find out, Rebecca will. An' she'll just edit for all she's worth!

"'The thought that God has planned it so/Should help us bear the years,'" Uncle Jerry read from the page Rebecca had left on the table. "Land, Mother, that takes right hold. How do you suppose she thought that out?"

"She couldn't have thought it out at her age," said Mrs. Cobb. "She must have guessed it was that way. We know some things without bein' told, Jeremiah."

&. &. &.

Rebecca took her scolding, which she richly deserved, like a soldier. There was considerable of it, and Miss Miranda remarked, among other things, that so absentminded a child was sure to grow up into a driveling idiot. She was bidden to stay away from Alice Robinson's birthday party and sentenced by Aunt Miranda to wear her dress, stained and streaked as it was, until it was worn out. Aunt Jane, however, eased Rebecca's pain by making her a ruffled apron artfully shaped to conceal all the spots. She was blessedly ready with these interventions between the poor little sinner and the full consequences of her sin, a circumstance which caused Rebecca to consider at times that Jesus had stood between her sin and the wrath of God. Yet this thought, in which she likened her aunts to Deity, she secretly supposed might be blasphemous.

However, Rebecca didn't mind staying away from Alice Robinson's party. She had told Emma Jane it would be like a picnic in a graveyard, since the Robinson house was as like a tomb as a house can manage to be. Children were commonly permitted to enter only at the back door, then required to stand on old newspapers while making their visit, so that Alice was begged by her friends to entertain them in the woodshed or barn whenever possible. Rebecca knew, also, that Mrs. Robinson was not only terribly neat but terribly stingy, so that the party refreshments were likely to be limited to peppermint drops and glasses of water.

13

SNOW WHITE
AND ROSE RED

O ne year just before Thanksgiving, the affairs of the
Simpsons reached a crisis. Riverboro was doing its
best to return the entire tribe of Simpsons to the land of its
fathers, thinking that the town which had given them birth,
rather than the town of their adoption, should feed them
and keep a roof over their heads until the children were of
an age for self-support.

Abner Simpson was in jail. This time his usual ninety
days had been extended to nine months by old Judge
Hingham. "You're a disgrace to the community and a bad
example to your children," the good judge had advised
him in an attempt to reach Simpson's conscience.

"Why, every town needs someone fer hypocrites t'
compare themselves to, Judge," Simpson countered.

"And your family—what are you doing for them?"

"Judge, no better father ever lived in the state of
Maine. Not only am I teachin' my kids sound business
principles, but by the time they are ready to fend fer themselves, they'll be s' clever the law won't bother 'em."

It is not known if Judge Hingham considered this contempt a jailworthy offense, or if he had simply tired of seeing Simpson before the bench for his swapping episodes. But he termed the case "habitual offender" and remanded him to the warden of York County Jail until well into the next summer.

With the Simpson family thus deprived of their breadwinner, and the northern winter coming on apace, there was little Riverboro's selectmen could do but bide their time. The Simpson's tumbledown house, caved-in barn, and three weedy acres had long since been acquired by the tax collector for nonpayment, making Mrs. Simpson and her brood full-fledged paupers and likely to become inmates of the poor farm unless the Town of Riverboro sustained them where they were domiciled. So First Selectman Bill Perkins dutifully engaged Abijah Flagg to cart enough board edgings from the sawmill for Mrs. Simpson to feed her stoves, keeping her children from freezing through the long Maine winter.

There was little to eat in the household and less to wear, though Mrs. Simpson did her poor best. The children often managed to satisfy their appetites by sitting modestly outside their neighbors' kitchen doors when meals were about to be served. They were not exactly popular favorites, but they did receive morsels of food from the more charitable housewives.

Life was rather dull and dreary, however. In the chill and gloom of November weather, with the vision of other people's turkeys bursting with fat and other people's golden pumpkins and squashes and corn being gathered into barns, the young Simpsons groped about for some inexpensive form of excitement, and they settled upon selling soap door-to-door to earn premiums. They had sold enough to their immediate neighbors during the earlier autumn to secure a child's handcart which could be trundled over the country roads to carry their wares. With large business sagacity which must have been inherited from their father, they now proposed to extend their operations to a wider area and distribute soap to nearby villages, if these villages could be induced to buy.

The Excelsior Soap Company paid a very small return to its agents, who were scattered through the state, but the company inflamed their imaginations by circulars with highly colored pictures of the premiums to be awarded for the sale of a certain number of cakes. Clara Belle and Susan Simpson consulted Rebecca, who threw herself wholeheartedly into the enterprise, promising her help and that of Emma Jane Perkins. The premiums within their possible grasp were two: a bookcase and a banquet lamp. The Simpsons had no books, so they warmed themselves rapturously in the vision of the banquet lamp, which speedily became to them more desirable than food, drink, or clothing.

Neither Emma Jane nor Rebecca saw anything unusual in the idea of the Simpsons striving for a banquet lamp. They looked at the picture daily and knew that if they themselves were free agents they would toil, suffer, sweat, for the happy privilege of occupying the same room with that lamp through the coming winter evenings. It looked to be about eight feet tall in the catalogue, and Emma Jane advised Clara Belle to measure the height of the Simpson ceilings. But a note in the margin of the circular informed them that it stood two-and-a-half feet high when set on a proper table, three dollars extra. It was only of polished brass, continued the circular, though it was invariably mistaken for solid gold, and the shade that accompanied it — if the agent sold a hundred extra cakes — was of crinkled crepe paper printed in a dozen delicious hues, from which the joy-dazzled agent might take his choice.

Seesaw Simpson was not in the soap syndicate. Clara Belle was a successful agent, but Susan, who could only say "thoap," never made large returns; and the twins, who were somewhat young to be thoroughly trustworthy, could be given only a half-dozen cakes at a time, and they were obliged to carry with them on their business trips a paper stating the price per cake, dozen, and box.

Rebecca and Emma Jane offered to go two or three miles in some direction and see what they could do in the way of stirring up a popular demand for Snow White laundry soap and Rose Red bath soap. There was a great amount of merriment in the preparation for Emma and Rebecca's sales trip and a long council in Emma Jane's attic. They had the soap company's circular from which to arrange a proper speech, and better still, the girls recalled a patent medicine vendor's speech at the Milltown Fair. His method could never be forgotten, nor his manner, nor his vocabulary. Emma Jane practiced it on Rebecca, and Rebecca on Emma Jane.

"Can I sell you a little soap this afternoon? It is called the Snow White and Rose Red Soap, six cakes in an ornamental box, only twenty cents for the white, twenty-five cents for the red. It is made from the purest ingredients, and, if desired, could be eaten by an invalid with relish and profit."

"Oh, Rebecca, don't let's say that!" interposed Emma Jane hysterically. "It makes me feel like a fool."

"It takes so little to make you feel like a fool, Emma Jane," rebuked Rebecca, "that sometimes I think that you must *be* one. I don't get to feeling like a fool so awfully easy. Now leave out that eating part if you don't like it, and go on."

"The Snow White is probably the most remarkable laundry soap ever manufactured. Immerse the garments in a tub, lightly rubbing the more soiled portions with the soap, leave them submerged in water from sunset to sunrise, and then the youngest baby can wash them without the slightest effort."

"Babe, not baby," corrected Rebecca from the circular.

"It's just the same thing," argued Emma Jane.

"Of course it's just the same *thing.* But a baby has got to be called babe or infant in a circular, the same as it is in poetry! Would you rather say infant?"

"No," grumbled Emma Jane. "Infant is worse even than babe. Rebecca, do you think we'd better do as the circular says and let Elijah or Elisha try the soap before we begin selling?"

"I can't imagine a babe doing a family wash with *any* soap," answered Rebecca. "But it must be true or they would never dare to print it, so don't let's bother. Oh! won't it be the greatest fun, Emma Jane? At some of the houses — where they can't possibly know me — I shan't be frightened, and I shall reel off the whole rigmarole, invalid, babe, and all. Perhaps I shall say even the last sentence, if I can remember it: 'We sound every chord in the great macrocosm of satisfaction.'"

This conversation took place on Friday afternoon at Emma Jane's house where Rebecca was to stay over Sunday, her aunts having gone to Portland to the funeral of an old friend. On Saturday they were going to use Mr. Perkins' old white horse, drive to North Riverboro three miles away, eat a twelve o'clock dinner with Emma Jane's cousins, and be back at four o'clock punctually.

Saturday was a glorious Indian summer day, which suggested nothing of Thanksgiving, near at hand as it was. It was a rustly day, a scarlet and buff, yellow and carmine, bronze and crimson day. There were still many leaves on the oaks and maples, making a goodly show of red and brown and gold. The air was like sparkling cider, and every field had its heaps of yellow and russet good things to eat, all ready for the barns, the mills, and the markets. The old horse forgot his twenty years, sniffed the sweet bright air, and trotted like a colt. Mt. Washington looked blue and clear in distant New Hampshire.

Rebecca stood in the wagon and created a poem about the landscape with sudden joy of living:

> Great, wide, beautiful, wonderful world,
> With the wonderful water round you curled,
> And the wonderful grass upon your breast,
> World, you are beautifully dressed.

Emma Jane had never seemed to Rebecca so near, so dear, so tried and true. And Rebecca, to Emma Jane's faithful heart, had never seemed so brilliant, so bewildering, so fascinating as in this visit together, with its freedom and the added delights of an exciting business enterprise.

A gorgeous leaf blew into the wagon. "Does color make you sort of dizzy?" asked Rebecca.

"No," answered Emma Jane after a long pause. "No, it doesn't, not a mite."

"Perhaps dizzy isn't just the right word, but it's nearest. I'd like to eat color and drink it and sleep in it. If you could be a tree, which one would you choose?"

"I'd rather be an apple tree in blossom, like the one that blooms pink by our pigpen."

Rebecca laughed. There was always something unexpected in Emma Jane's replies. "I'd choose to be that scarlet maple just on the edge of the pond there"—and she pointed with the horsewhip. "Then I could see so much

more than your pink apple tree by the pigpen. I could look
at all the rest of the woods, see my scarlet dress in my
beautiful water looking glass, and watch all the yellow and
brown trees growing upside down in the water. When I'm
old enough to earn money, I'm going to have a dress like
this leaf, all ruby color—thin, you know, with a sweeping
train and ruffly curly edges. Then I think I'll have a brown
sash like the trunk of the tree. And where could I be
green? Do they have green petticoats, I wonder? I'd like a
green petticoat coming out now and then underneath to
show what my leaves were like before I was a scarlet
maple."

"I think it would be awful homely," said Emma Jane.
"I'm going to have a white satin dress with a pink sash,
pink stockings, bronze slippers, and a spangled fan."

14

MR. ALADDIN

The girls did not accompany each other to the doors of their chosen customers, feeling sure that together they could not approach selling seriously. Rather, they parted at the gate of each house, the one holding the horse while the other took the soap samples and made her pitch to anyone who seemed of a coming-on disposition. Emma Jane had sold three single cakes, Rebecca three small boxes, for a difference in their ability to persuade the public was obvious from the start, though neither of them ascribed either success or defeat to anything but the circumstances. Housewives looked at Emma Jane and desired no soap, listened to her describe its merits, and still they desired none.

Other stars in their courses governed Rebecca's doings. The people she interviewed either remembered their present need of soap or reminded themselves that they would need it in the future. Rebecca accomplished with almost no effort results that poor Emma Jane failed to attain by hard and conscientious labor.

"It's your turn, Rebecca, and I'm glad, too," said Emma Jane, drawing the horse and wagon up to a gateway and pointing out a house far from the road. "I haven't got over trembling from the last place, yet." (A lady had put her head out of an upstairs window and called, "Go away, girl. Whatever you have in your box we don't want any.") "I don't know who lives here, and the blinds are all shut in front. If there's nobody at home you musn't count it, but take the next house as yours, too."

Rebecca walked up the long lane and went to the side door. There was a porch there, and seated in a rocking chair husking corn was a good-looking young man. He had an air of the city about him — well-shaven face, well-trimmed mustache, well-fitting, tailored clothes. Rebecca was a trifle shy at this unexpected encounter, but there was nothing to be done but explain her presence, so she asked, "Is the lady of the house at home?"

"I am the lady of the house at present," said the stranger with a disarming smile. "What can I do for you?"

"Have you ever heard of the. . .would you like, or I mean. . .do you need any soap?" questioned Rebecca.

"Do I look as if I did?" he responded unexpectedly.

Rebecca dimpled. "I didn't mean *that.* I have some soap to sell. I mean I would like to introduce to you a very remarkable soap, the best on the market. It is called the . . ."

"Oh, I know that soap," said the gentleman genially. "Made out of pure vegetable oils, isn't it?"

"The very purest," agreed Rebecca.

"No acid in it?"

"Not a trace."

"And a child could do the Monday washing with it and use no force."

"A babe," corrected Rebecca.

"Oh! a babe, eh? That child grows younger every year instead of older — wise child!"

This was great fortune, to find a customer who knew all the virtues of the product in advance. Rebecca dimpled more and more, and at her new friend's invitation she sat down on a stool at his side near the edge of the porch. The beauties of the ornamental box which held the Rose Red bath soap were disclosed, and the prices of both that and the Snow White laundry soap were unfolded. Presently she forgot all about her silent partner at the gate and was talking as if she had known this grand person all her life.

"I'm keeping house today, but I don't live here," explained the delightful gentleman. "I'm just on a visit to my aunt, who has gone to Portland for the day. I used to live here as a boy, and I am very fond of the spot, so I do come back for a week now and then."

"I don't think anything takes the place of the farm where one lived when one was a child," observed Rebecca, extremely pleased at having found that the citified stranger agreed with her tastes in lifestyles.

The man darted a look at her and put down his ear of corn. "So you consider your childhood a thing of the past, do you, young lady?"

"I can still remember it," answered Rebecca gravely, "though it seems a long time ago."

"I can remember mine well enough, and a particularly unpleasant one it was," said the stranger sadly.

"So was mine," agreed Rebecca, quickly adding, "we were happy enough on our farm until my father died. What was *your* worst trouble?"

"Lack of food and clothes, principally."

"Oh!" exclaimed Rebecca with sympathetic understanding. "Mine was no shoes and not enough books. But you're all right and happy now, aren't you?" she asked doubtfully, for though he looked handsome, well-fed, and prosperous, any child could see that his eyes were tired and his mouth was sad when he was not speaking.

"I'm doing pretty well, thank you," said the man with a delightful smile. "Now tell me, how much soap ought I to buy today?"

"How much has your aunt on hand now?" suggested the very modest and inexperienced agent, "and how much would she need?"

"Oh, I don't know about that. Soap keeps, doesn't it?"

"I'm not certain," said Rebecca conscientiously, "but I'll look in the circular — it's sure to tell." She drew the document from her pocket.

"What are you going to do with the magnificent profits from this business?"

"We are not selling for our own benefit," said Rebecca confidentially. "My friend who is holding the horse at the gate is the daughter of a prosperous blacksmith, and she really doesn't need the money. I live with my aunts in the brick house in Riverboro. They're kind of stuffy, so they wouldn't like me to be a peddler. We are trying to get a premium for some friends of ours."

Unexpectedly, Rebecca found herself describing Mr. Simpson, Mrs. Simpson, and the Simpson family — their poverty, their joyless life, and their abject need of a banquet lamp to brighten their evenings, lighted only by the cheapest of tallow candles.

"You needn't argue that point," laughed the man, as he stood up to get a glimpse of the "rich blacksmith's daughter" at the gate. "I can see that they ought to have it if they want it. I've known what it was myself to do without a banquet lamp. Now give me the circular, and let's do some figuring. How much do the Simpsons lack at this moment?"

"If they sell 200 more cakes this month, they can have the lamp by Christmas," Rebecca answered. "And they can get a shade by summertime. But I'm afraid I can't help very much after today, because my Aunt Miranda may not like to have me."

"I see. Well, that's all right. I'll take 300 cakes, and that will give them the lamp, shade and all."

Rebecca had been seated on a stool very near the edge of the porch, and at this remark she made a sudden movement, tipped over, and disappeared into a clump of lilac bushes. It was a very short distance, fortunately, and the amused stranger picked her up, set her on her feet, and brushed her off. "You should never seem surprised when you have taken a large order," said he. "You ought to have replied, 'Can't you make it 350?' instead of capsizing in that unbusinesslike way."

"Oh, I could never say anything like that!" exclaimed Rebecca, who was blushing crimson at her awkward fall. "But it doesn't seem right for you to buy so much. Are you sure you can afford it?"

"If I can't, I'll save on something else," returned the jolly philanthropist.

"What if your aunt shouldn't like this kind of soap?" queried Rebecca nervously.

"My aunt always likes what I like," he returned.

"Mine doesn't!" exclaimed Rebecca.

"Then there's something wrong with your aunt!"

"Or with me," laughed Rebecca.

"What is your name, young lady?"

"Rebecca Rowena Randall, sir."

"What?" he cried with an amused smile. *"Both?* Your mother was generous."

"She couldn't bear to give up either of the names, she says."

"Do you want to hear my name?"

"I think I know it already," answered Rebecca with a bright glance. "I'm sure you must be Mr. Aladdin from the

*. . . she made a sudden movement, tipped over,
and disappeared into a clump of lilac bushes.*

Arabian Nights. Oh, please can I run and tell Emma Jane? She must be so tired waiting, and she will be so glad!" At the man's nod of assent, Rebecca sped down the lane, shouting irrepressibly as she neared the wagon, "Oh, Emma Jane! Emma Jane! We are sold out!"

Mr. Aladdin followed smilingly to corroborate this astonishing, unbelievable statement. He lifted all the soap boxes from the back of the wagon, and taking the circular, promised to write to the Excelsior Soap Company that very evening himself concerning the Simpson's lamp.

"If you could contrive to keep a secret, you two girls, it would be rather a nice surprise to have the lamp arrive at the Simpsons on Thanksgiving Day, wouldn't it?" he asked, as he tucked the old buffalo lap robe cozily over their feet.

They gladly agreed and thanked him excitedly as tears of joy stood in Rebecca's eyes.

"Oh, don't mention it!" laughed Mr. Aladdin, lifting his hat in a courteous salute. "I was sort of a traveling salesman myself once, years ago, and I like to see the thing well done. Good-by, Miss Rebecca Rowena! Just let me know whenever you have anything to sell, for I'm certain beforehand I shall want it."

"Good-by, Mr. Aladdin! I surely will!" cried Rebecca, tossing back her dark braids delightedly and waving her hand.

"Oh, Rebecca," said Emma Jane in an awestruck whisper. "He raised his hat to us, and we are not even fourteen! It'll be years before we're ladies."

"Never mind," answered Rebecca. "We are the *beginnings* of ladies, even now."

"He tucked the lap robe around us, too," continued Emma Jane in ecstasy. "Oh, isn't he perfectly elergant? And wasn't it lovely of him to buy us out? And just think of having both the lamp and the shade for one day's work! Aren't you glad you wore your pink gingham now, even if Mother did make you put on flannel underneath? You do look so pretty in pink and red, Rebecca, and so homely in drab and brown!"

"I know it," sighed Rebecca. "I wish I was like you — pretty in all colors!" And Rebecca looked longingly at Emma Jane's round, rosy cheeks, at her blue eyes, at her neat nose, at her red lips.

"Never mind!" said Emma Jane, comfortingly. "Everybody says you're awful bright and smart, and Mother thinks you'll be better looking all the time as you grow older. You wouldn't believe it, but I was a dreadful homely baby, and homely right along until a couple of years ago when I began to grow and my red hair began to grow dark. What was that nice man's name?"

"I never thought to ask!" exclaimed Rebecca. "Aunt Miranda would say that was just like me, and it is. But I called him Mr. Aladdin because he gave us a lamp. You know the story of Aladdin and the wonderful lamp?"

"Oh, Rebecca! How could you call him a nickname the very first time you ever saw him?"

"Aladdin isn't a nickname, exactly. Anyway, he laughed and seemed to like it."

On Thanksgiving Day, Jeremiah Cobb, who drove the mail coach, delivered the lamp to the Simpsons in a large, wooden packing box. It was taken out and set up by Seesaw, who suddenly began to admire and respect the business ability of his sisters.

Rebecca had heard the news of its arrival, but she waited until nearly dark before asking permission to go to the Simpsons so that she might see the gorgeous trophy lighted and sending a blaze of crimson glory from its kerosene wick through the red crepe paper shade.

15

THE BANQUET LAMP

There had been company at the brick house for the bountiful Thanksgiving dinner which had been provided at one o'clock — the Burnham sisters, who lived between North Riverboro and Shaker Village, and who for more than a quarter century had come to pass the holiday with the Sawyers every year.

Rebecca sat silent with a book after the dinner dishes were washed, and when it was nearly five, she asked if she might go to the Simpsons'.

"What do you want to run after those Simpson children for on Thanksgiving Day?" queried Miss Miranda. "Can't you set still for once and listen to the improvin' conversation of your elders? You never can let well enough alone but want to be forever on the move."

"The Simpsons have a new lamp, and Emma Jane and I promised to go up and see it lighted and make it kind of a party."

"What under the sun did they want of a lamp, and where did they get the money to pay for it? If Abner weren't in jail, I should think he'd been swappin' again," said Miss Miranda.

"The children got it as a prize for selling soap," replied Rebecca. "They've been working for a year, and you know I told you that Emma Jane and I helped them the Saturday afternoon you were in Portland."

"I didn't take notice, I suppose, for it's the first time I ever heard the lamp mentioned. Well, you can go for an hour and no more. Remember, it's as dark at six as it is at midnight this time o' year. Would you like to take along some Baldwin apples? What have you got in the pocket of that new dress that makes it sag down so?"

"It's my nuts and raisins from dinner," replied Rebecca, who never succeeded in keeping the most innocent action a secret from her Aunt Miranda. "They're just what you gave me on my plate."

"Why didn't you eat them?"

"Because I'd had enough dinner, and I thought if I saved these, it would make the Simpsons' party better," stammered Rebecca, who hated to be scolded and examined before company.

"They are your own, Rebecca," interposed Aunt Jane, "and if you choose to save them to give away, it is all right. We ought never to let this day pass without giving our neighbors something to be thankful for instead of taking all the time to think of our own mercies."

The Burnham sisters nodded approvingly as Rebecca went out, and remarked that they had never seen a child grow and improve so fast in so short a time.

"There's plenty of room left for more improvement, as you'd know if she lived in the same house with you," answered Miranda. "She's into everything in the neighborhood, an' not only into it, but generally at the head an' front of it, especially when it's mischief. Of all the foolishness I ever heard of, that lamp beats everything. It's just like those Simpsons, but I didn't suppose the children had brains enough to sell anything."

"One of them must have," said Miss Ellen Burnham, "for the girl that was selling soap at the Ladds in North Riverboro was described by Adam Ladd as the most remarkable and winning young lady he ever saw."

"It must have been Clara Belle, but I should never call her remarkable," answered Miss Miranda. "Has Adam been home again?"

"Yes, he's been staying a few days with his aunt. There's no limit to the money he's making, they say, and he always brings presents for all the neighbors. This time it was a full set of furs for Mrs. Ladd. And to think we can remember the time he was a barefoot boy without two shirts to his back! It is strange he hasn't married, with all his money from the railroad business, and him so fond of children that he always has a pack of them at his heels."

"There's hope for him still, though," said Miss Jane smilingly, "for I don't suppose he's more than twenty-three or -four."

"He could get a wife in Riverboro if he was a hundred and twenty four," remarked Miss Miranda.

"Adam's aunt says he was so taken with the girl that sold the soap—Clara Belle, did you say her name was?— that he declared he was going to bring her a Christmas present," continued Miss Ellen.

"Well, there's no accountin' for tastes," exclaimed Miss Miranda. "Clara Belle's got cross-eyes and red hair, but I'd be the last one to grudge her a Christmas present. The more Adam Ladd gives to her the less the town'll have to."

"Isn't there another Simpson girl?" asked Miss Lydia Burnham. "This one couldn't have been cross-eyed. I remember Mrs. Ladd saying Adam remarked about this child's handsome eyes. He said it was her eyes that made him buy the 300 cakes. Mrs. Ladd has it stacked up in the shed chamber."

Miranda gasped. "Did you say 300 cakes? Well, there's one crop that never fails in Riverboro!"

"What's that?" asked Miss Lydia politely.

"The fool crop," responded Miranda tersely, and she changed the subject, much to Jane's gratitude, for she had been nervous and ill at ease for the last fifteen minutes. What child in Riverboro could be described as remarkable and winning, save Rebecca? What child had wonderful eyes, except the same Rebecca? And finally, was there ever a child in the world who could make a man buy soap — 300 cakes of it — save Rebecca?

⁖ ⁖ ⁖

Meantime, the "remarkable" young lady had flown up the road in the deepening dusk, but she had not gone far before she heard the sound of hurrying footsteps and saw a well-known figure coming in her direction. In a moment she and Emma Jane met and exchanged a breathless embrace.

"Something awful has happened," panted Emma Jane.

"Don't tell me it's broken," exclaimed Rebecca.

"No! Oh, no! Not that! It was packed in straw, and every piece came out all right. And I was there, and I never said a single thing about your selling the 300 cakes that got the lamp, so that we could be together when you told."

"*Our* selling the 300 cakes," corrected Rebecca. "You did as much as I."

"No, I didn't, Rebecca Randall. I just sat at the gate and held the horse."

"Yes, but *whose* horse was it that took us to North Riverboro? And besides, it just happened to be my turn. If you had gone in and found Mr. Aladdin, you would have had the wonderful lamp given to you. But what's the trouble?"

"The Simpsons have no kerosene, since they light with candles. I guess they thought a banquet lamp was something that lighted itself and burned without any help. Mother let me have a pint of coal oil, but she says she won't give me any more. We never thought of the expense of keeping up the lamp, Rebecca. Kerosene is fifteen cents a gallon!"

"Aunt Jane says that kerosene's cheaper than candles, once you own a lamp," said Rebecca thoughtfully. "That's why she bought me a small lamp for my bedroom last year; it cost a whole dollar, too. But let's not worry about the price of lamp oil till after the party. I have a handful of nuts and raisins, and some apples which Aunt Miranda sent."

"I have peppermints and maple sugar," said Emma Jane. "They had a real Thanksgiving dinner. The doctor gave them sweet potatoes and cranberries and turnips. Father sent a sparerib roast, and Mrs. Cobb a chicken and a jar of mincemeat for pie."

At half past five one might have looked in at the Simpsons' windows and have seen the party at its height. Mrs. Simpson had let the kitchen fire die out and had brought the baby to grace the festal scene. The lamp seemed to be having the party and receiving the guests. The children had taken the one small table in the house, and it was placed in the center of the room to serve as a pedestal. On it stood the adored, the long-desired object, almost as beautiful and nearly half as large as the advertisement. The brass glistened like gold, and the crimson paper shade glowed like a giant ruby.

In the wide splash of light that the lamp flung upon the floor sat the Simpsons in reverent and solemn silence,

Emma Jane standing behind them, hand in hand with Rebecca. There seemed to be no desire for conversation. The
occasion was too thrilling and serious for that. The lamp, it
was felt by everybody, was dignifying the party and provid-
ing sufficient entertainment simply by its presence, being
fully as satisfactory in its way as a piano or a string band.

"I wish Father could see it," said Clara Belle loyally.

"If he once thaw it he'd want to thwap it," murmured
Susan sagaciously.

At the appointed hour, Rebecca dragged herself reluctantly away from the enchanting scene.

"I'll blow the lamp out the minute I think you and
Emma Jane are home," said Clara Belle. "And oh, I'm so
glad you both live where you can see it shine through our
windows. I wonder how long it will burn without bein'
filled if I only keep it lit one hour every night?"

"You needn't put it out for want o' kerosene," said
Seesaw, coming in from the woodshed, "for there's a great
keg of it settin' out there. Mr. Watson brought it over from
his store. He said somebody sent an order by mail for it."

Rebecca squeezed Emma Jane's arm, and Emma Jane
gave a rapturous return squeeze. "It was Mr. Aladdin,"
whispered Rebecca, as they ran down the path to the gate.
Seesaw followed them and offered to see them a piece
down the road, but Rebecca declined his escort with such
decision that he did not press the matter but went home to
bed to dream of her instead.

Rebecca entered the home dining room joyously. The
Burnham sisters had gone, and the two aunts were knitting. "It was a heavenly party," she cried, taking off her
hat and cape.

"Go back and see if you have shut the door tight, and
then lock it," said Miss Miranda, in her usual austere manner.

"It *was* a heavenly party," reiterated Rebecca, coming back in again, much too excited to be easily crushed. "And oh, Aunt Jane, Aunt Miranda, if you'll only come into the kitchen and look out of the sink window you can see the banquet lamp shining all red, just as if the Simpsons' house was on fire."

"And probably it will be before long," observed Miranda. "I've got no patience with such foolish goin's-on an' children playin' with an oil lamp!"

Jane accompanied Rebecca into the kitchen. Although the glimmer which she was able to see from that distance did not seem to her a dazzling exhibition, she tried to be as enthusiastic as possible.

"Rebecca, who was it that sold the 300 cakes of soap to Mr. Ladd in North Riverboro?"

"Mr. *Who?*" exclaimed Rebecca.

"Mr. Ladd, in North Riverboro."

"Is that his real name?" queried Rebecca in astonishment. "I didn't make a bad guess." And she laughed softly to herself.

"I asked you who sold the soap to Adam Ladd?" resumed Miss Jane.

"Adam Ladd! Then he's A. Ladd, too! What fun!"

"Answer me, Rebecca."

"Oh, excuse me, Aunt Jane. I was so busy thinking. Emma Jane and I sold the soap to Mr. Ladd."

"Did you tease him or make him buy it?"

"Now, Aunt Jane, how could I make a grown-up man buy anything if he didn't want to? He needed the soap dreadfully as a present for his aunt."

Miss Jane still looked a little unconvinced, though she only said, "I hope your Aunt Miranda won't mind. You know how particular she is, Rebecca, and I really wish you wouldn't do anything out of the ordinary without asking her first, for your actions are very queer."

"There can't be anything wrong this time," Rebecca answered confidently. "Emma Jane sold her cakes to her own relations and to Uncle Jerry and Aunt Sarah, and I went first to those new tenements near the lumber mill, and then to the Ladds. Mr. Ladd bought all we had and made us promise to keep the secret until the premium came, and I've been going about ever since as if the banquet lamp was inside of me all lighted up and burning for everybody to see."

Rebecca's hair was loosened and falling over her forehead in ruffled waves; her eyes were brilliant, her cheeks were crimson; there was a hint of everything in the girl's face — of sensitiveness and delicacy as well as of ardor. There was the sweetness of the mayflower and the strength of the young oak, but one could easily divine that she was one of

> The souls by nature pitched too high,
> By suffering plunged too low.

"That's just the way you look, for all the world as if you did have a lamp burning inside of you," sighed Aunt Jane. "Rebecca! Rebecca! I wish you could take things easier, child. I am fearful for you sometimes."

16

DEACON ISRAEL'S SUCCESSOR

There was an event that made a deep impression in several quarters and left a wake of smaller events in its train. This was the coming to Riverboro of Amos Burch and wife, returned missionaries from Africa.

The Missionary Aid Society had called its meeting for a Wednesday in March. It was a raw, blustering day, snow on the ground, and a look in the sky of more to follow. Both Miranda and Jane had taken cold and decided that they could not leave the house in such weather, and this worried Miranda since she was an officer of the society.

After making the breakfast table sufficiently uncomfortable and wishing plaintively that Jane wouldn't always insist on being sick at the same time she was, Miranda decided that Rebecca must go to the meeting in their stead.

"You'll be better than nobody, Rebecca," she said flatteringly. "Your Aunt Jane shall write an excuse from afternoon school for you. You can wear your rubber boots and come home by the way of the church meetin' house. This Mr. Burch, if I remember right, used to know your Grandfather Sawyer and stayed here once when he was a young candidate for missionary service. He'll mebbe look for us there, and you must just go and represent the family an' give him our respects. Be careful how you behave. Tell everybody what awful colds we've got. If you see a good chance, take your pocket handkerchief and wipe the dust off the pump organ before the meetin' begins, and get twenty-five cents out of the sittin' room matchbox in case there should be a collection."

Rebecca willingly assented; the idea of representing the family was especially intoxicating.

The service was held in a Sunday school room. Mr. Burch was on the platform when Rebecca entered, and there were a dozen ladies present. Feeling a little shy and too young for this gathering, Rebecca sought the shelter of a friendly face. Seeing Mrs. Robinson in one of the side seats near the front, she walked up the aisle and sat beside her.

"Both my aunts had bad colds," she said softly, "and they sent me to represent the family."

"That's Mrs. Burch on the platform with her husband," whispered Mrs. Robinson. "She's awful tanned up, ain't she? If you're goin' to be a missionary, seems like you have to part with your complexion. Eudoxy Morton ain't come yet. I hope she will, or Miz Deacon Milliken'll pitch the tunes where we can't reach 'em with a ladder. Can't you pitch afore she gits her breath and clears her throat?"

Mrs. Burch was a slim, frail little woman with dark hair, a broad forehead, and patient mouth. She was dressed in a well-worn black silk and looked so tired that Rebecca's heart went out to her.

"They're poor as Job's turkey," whispered Mrs. Robinson, "but if you give 'em anything, they'd turn right 'round and give it to the heathen. His congregation up to East Parsonsfield clubbed together and give him that gold watch he carries. I s'pose he'da handed that over too, only heathens always tell time by the sun 'n' don't need watches. Eudoxy ain't comin' — now for massy's sake, Rebecca, do git ahead of Miz Deacon Milliken and pitch real low."

Church of our God! arise and shine,
Bright with the beams of truth divine:
Then shall thy radiance stream afar,
Wide as the heathen nations are.
Gentiles and kings thy light shall view,
And shall admire and love thee too.

"Is there anyone present who will assist us at the organ?" Mr. Burch asked unexpectedly.

Everybody looked at everybody else, and nobody moved. Then there came a voice out of a far corner saying informally, "Rebecca, why don't you?" It was Mrs. Cobb. Rebecca could have played in the dark, so she went to the old organ and did so without any ado, no member of her family being present to give her self-consciousness.

The talk that ensued was much the usual sort of thing. Mr. Burch made impassioned appeals for the spreading of the gospel, and he added his entreaties that all who were prevented from visiting in person the peoples who sat in darkness should contribute to the support of others who could go, as well as pray for them each day. But he did more than this. Burch was a pleasant, earnest speaker, and he interwove his discourse with stories of life in a foreign land — of the manners, the customs, the speech, the point of view — even giving glimpses of the daily round, the common task, of his own household, the work of his devoted helpmate and their little group of children, all born under African skies.

Rebecca sat entranced, having been given the key to another world. Riverboro had faded. The Sunday school room, with Mrs. Robinson's red plaid shawl, and Deacon

Milliken's wife, with her wig on crooked, the bare benches
and worn hymnbooks, the hanging texts and maps of Bible
lands, was no longer visible. She saw instead blue skies
and burning stars, white turbans and gay colors, thatched
huts of mud bricks, village compounds where skinny
roosters crow from the walls at dawn. Mr. Burch had not
said so, but perhaps there were mosques and minarets and
palm trees. What stories they must know, those children
born under African skies! Then she was called upon to
play "Jesus shall reign where'er the sun."

The contribution box was passed, and Mr. Burch
prayed. As he opened his eyes and gave out the last hymn,
he looked at the handful of people, at the scattered pennies
and dimes in the contribution box, and reflected that his
mission was not only to gather funds for the building of
his church beyond the seas, but to keep alive in all these
remote and lonely Maine neighborhoods a love for the
cause which was its only hope in the years to come.

"If any of the sisters will provide entertainment," he
said, "Mrs. Burch and I will remain among you tonight
and tomorrow. Then we could hold a parlor meeting in
one of your homes. My wife and one of my children will
wear the native costume. We would display some speci-
mens of African handiwork and give an account of our
educational methods with the children. These informal parlor meetings, admitting of questions or conversation, are
often the means of interesting those not commonly found
at church services. So I repeat, if any member of the congregation desires it and offers her hospitality, we will
gladly stay and tell you more of the Lord's work."

Silence settled over the little assembly. There was
some cogent reason why every "sister" there was disin-
clined for company. Some had no spare room; some had a
pantry less well stocked than usual. Some had sickness in

the family; some had husbands who disliked strange ministers. Mrs. Burch's thin hands fingered her black silk nervously. *Would no one speak!* thought Rebecca, her heart
fluttering with sympathy.

Mrs. Robinson leaned over and whispered signifi-
cantly, "The missionaries always used to be entertained at
the brick house. Your grandfather never would let 'em
sleep anywheres else when he was alive."

She meant this for a stab at Miss Miranda's stinginess,
remembering the four spare bedrooms, closed from January to December. But Rebecca thought it was intended as
a suggestion. If it had once been a custom, perhaps her
aunts would want her to do the right thing, for why else
was she representing the family? So, delighted that duty
lay in so pleasant a direction, she rose from her seat and
said in a pretty voice and with the quaint, polite manner
that so separated her from all the other young people in
the village, "My aunts, Miss Miranda and Miss Jane Sawyer, would be very happy to have you visit them at the
brick house, as the ministers always used to do when their
father was alive. They sent their respects by me."

Mr. Burch bowed courteously, accepted the invitation
"in the same spirit in which it was offered," and then
closed the meeting in prayer.

In a moment or two, when the room began to clear,
Rebecca went up to Mrs. Burch, who kissed her affection-
ately and said, "My dear, how glad I am that we are going
to stay with you. Will half past five be too late for us to
come? It is three now, and we have to go to the station for
our bags and for our children. We left them there, being
uncertain whether we should go back or stop here."

Rebecca said that half past five was their supper hour
and then accepted an invitation to drive home with Mrs.
Cobb in her top buggy. She entered the brick house cheer-

ily, the distant hoofbeats of Aunt Sarah Cobb's mare beating in time with her excited heart on the plank bridge beneath the hill. Being too full of news to wait in the side entry to take off her rubber boots, she carefully lifted a braided rug into the sitting room and stood on that while she opened her report.

"There are your shoes warming by the fire," said Aunt Jane pleasantly. "Slip them right on while you talk."

"It was a very small meeting, Aunt Miranda," began Rebecca, "and the missionary and his wife are lovely people, and they are coming here to stay all night and tomorrow with you. I hope you won't mind."

"Coming here!" exclaimed Miranda, letting her knitting fall in her lap and taking her spectacles off as she always did in moments of extreme excitement. "Did they invite themselves?"

"No," Rebecca answered. "I had to invite them for you, but I thought you'd like to have such interesting company. It was this way . . ."

"Stop your explainin' and tell me first when they'll be here. Right away?"

"No, not for two hours—about half past five."

"Then you can explain, if you can, who gave you authority to invite a passel of strangers to stop here overnight when you know we ain't had any company for twenty years and don't intend to have any for another twenty—or at any rate, while I'm the head of the house."

"Don't blame her, Miranda, till you've heard her story," said Jane softly. "It was in my mind right along, that if we went to the meeting some such thing might happen, on account of Mr. Burch knowing Father."

"The meeting was a small one," began Rebecca. "I gave all your messages, and everybody was disappointed you couldn't come, for the president wasn't there, and

Mrs. Matthews took the chair, which was a pity, for the seat wasn't nearly big enough for her; and she reminded me of a line in a hymn we sang, 'Wide as the heathen nations are,' and she wore that kind of a beaver garden hat that always gets on one side. And Mr. Burch talked beautifully about the African heathen, and the singing went real well, and there looked to be about forty cents in the basket that was passed on our side. And that wouldn't save even a heathen baby, would it?

"Then Mr. Burch said, if any sister would offer entertainment, they would pass the night and have a parlor meeting in Riverboro tomorrow, with Mrs. Burch in African costume and lovely foreign things to show. Then he waited and waited, and nobody said a word. I was so mortified I didn't know what to do. And then he repeated what he said and explained why he wanted to stay, and you could see he thought the Lord was leadin' him to stay in Riverboro.

"Just then Mrs. Robinson whispered to me and said the missionaries always used to go to the brick house when Grandfather Israel Sawyer was alive and that he never would let them sleep anywhere else. I didn't know you had stopped having them, because no traveling ministers have been here except just for a Sunday morning since I came to Riverboro. So I thought I ought to invite them as you weren't there to do it. For you yourself told me to represent the family."

"What did you do—go up and introduce yourself as folks was goin' out?"

"No, I stood right up in meeting. I had to, for Mr. Burch's feelings were getting hurt at nobody's speaking. So I said, 'My aunts, Miss Miranda and Miss Jane Sawyer, would be happy to have you visit at the brick house, just as the missionaries always did when their father was alive,

and they sent their respects by me.' Then I sat down, and
Mr. Burch prayed and called Grandfather a man of God,
and thanked our Heavenly Father that his spirit was still
alive in his descendants, and that the good old house
where so many of the brethren had been cheered and
helped, and from which so many had gone out strength-
ened for the fight, was still hospitably open for the
stranger and wayfarer."

A certain gateway in Miranda Sawyer's soul had been
closed for years. Not all at once had it been done, but
gradually, and without her full knowledge. If Rebecca had
plotted for days and with the utmost cunning, she could
not have effected an entrance into that forbidden country.
Yet now, unknown to both of them, the gate swung on its
stiff and rusty hinges, and the favoring wind of opportunity opened it wider and wider as time went on.

All things had worked together amazingly for good.
The memory of old days had been evoked, and the daily
life of a godly and venerated father called to mind. The
Sawyer name had been publicly dignified and praised, Rebecca had comported herself as the granddaughter of Deacon Israel Sawyer should and showed conclusively that
she was not "all Randall," as had been supposed. Miranda
was rather soothed by and pleased with the turn of events,
although she did not intend to show it or give anybody
any reason to expect that this expression of hospitality was
to serve as a precedent.

"Well, I see you did only what you was obliged to do,
Rebecca," she said, "and you worded your invitation as
nice as anybody could have done. I wish your Aunt Jane
and me wasn't so worthless with these colds, but it only
shows the good of havin' a clean house, with every room
in order, whether open or shut, and enough vittles cooked
so't you can't be surprised and belittled by anybody, what-

ever happens. There was half a dozen there that might have entertained the Burches as easy as not, if they hadn'ta been too mean or lazy. Why didn't the missionaries come right along with you?"

"They had to go to the station for their bags and their children."

"Are there children?" worried Miranda.

"Yes, Aunt Miranda, all born under African skies."

"How many?"

"I didn't think to ask, but I will get two rooms ready, and if there are any over, I'll take 'em into my bed," said Rebecca, secretly hoping that this would be the case. "Now, as you're both half sick, couldn't you trust me just once to get ready for the company? You can come up when I call. Will you?"

"I believe I will," sighed Miranda reluctantly. "I'll lay down 'side o' Jane in our bedroom and see if I can get strength to cook supper. It's half past three — don't you let me lay a minute past five. I kep' a good fire in the kitchen stove. I don't know, I'm sure, why I should have baked a pot o' beans in the middle of the week, but they'll come in handy. Father used to say there was nothing that went right to the spot with returned missionaries like pork 'n' beans 'n' brown bread. Fix up the two south chambers, Rebecca."

17

THE HOSTESS
OF THE BRICK HOUSE

R ebecca, given a free hand in the brick house for the
first time in her life, dashed upstairs like a whirl-
wind. Every room in the brick house was as neat as wax,
and she had only to pull up the shades, go over the floors
lightly with a broom, and dust the furniture. The aunts
could hear her scurrying to and fro, fluffing up pillows and
feather beds, flapping towels, jingling chamber pots and
wash basins, singing meanwhile in her clear voice:

> Where Afric's sunny fountains
> Roll down their golden sand:
> What though the spicy breezes
> Blow soft o'er, Ceylon's isle;
> Where every prospect pleases,
> And only man is vile

> In vain with lavish kindness
> The gifts of God are strown;
> The heathen in his blindness
> Bows down to wood and stone.

Rebecca had grown to be a handy little creature, and tasks she was capable of doing, she did like a flash, so that when she called her aunts at five o'clock to pass judgment, she had accomplished wonders. There were fresh towels on bureaus, and lamps were filled, and soap and matches were laid out; newspaper, kindling, and wood were in the boxes, and a large stick burned slowly in each airtight stove. "I thought I'd better just take the chill off," she explained, "as they're right from Africa, and that reminds me, I must look it up in the geography before they get here."

There was nothing to disapprove, so the two sisters went downstairs to make some slight changes in their dress. As they passed the sitting room door, Miranda thought she heard a crackle and looked in. The shades were up, and a cheerful blaze glowed through the isinglass window in front of the black iron stove. Aunt Miranda's best kerosene lamp, a nickel-plated brass Rochester, stood on a marble-topped table in the corner. The light that came softly through its rose-colored shade transformed the stiff and gloomy ugliness of the room into a place where one could sit and love one's neighbor.

"For massy's sake, Rebecca," called Miss Miranda up the stairs, "did you think we'd better open the sitting room in cold weather? The dining room ought to be large enough, hadn't it?"

Rebecca came out on the landing braiding her hair.

"We did on Thanksgiving and Christmas, and I thought this was about as great an occasion," she said. "I moved the wax flowers off the mantelpiece so they wouldn't melt and put the shells, the coral, and the green stuffed bird on top of the bookcase, so the children wouldn't ask to play with them. Brother Milliken's coming over to see Mr. Burch about business, and I shouldn't wonder if Brother and Sister Cobb happened in. Don't go down cellar. I'll be there in a minute to do the running."

Miranda and Jane exchanged glances.

"Ain't she the beatin'est creeture that ever was born into the world!" exclaimed Miranda. "My, but she can turn out work when she's got a mind to!"

At quarter past five everything was ready, and the neighbors, those at least who were within sight of the brick house — a prominent object in the landscape when there were no leaves on the trees — were curious almost to desperation. Shades up in the sitting room! Shades up in the two south bedrooms! And fires — if human vision was to be relied on — fires in about every room. If it had not been for a lady who had been at the meeting who called in at one or two houses and explained the reason of all this preparation, there would have been no sleep in many Riverboro families that night.

The missionary family arrived promptly, and there were but two children, the other three having been left in Portland to diminish traveling expenses. Jane escorted them all upstairs, while Miranda watched the cooking of the supper. But Rebecca promptly took the two little girls away from their mother, divested them of their wraps, smoothed their hair, and brought them down to the kitchen to smell the beans.

There was a bountiful supper, and the presence of the young people robbed it of all possible stiffness. Aunt Jane helped clear the table and put away the food, while Miranda entertained in the sitting room, but Rebecca and the little Burches washed the dishes and held high carnival in the kitchen, doing only trifling damage: breaking a cup and plate that had been cracked before, emptying a silver spoon with some dishwater out of the back door, and putting coffee grounds in the sink. All evidences of crime having been removed by Rebecca, and damages repaired in all possible cases, the three entered the sitting room, where Mr. and Mrs. Cobb and Deacon and Mrs. Milliken had already appeared.

It was such a pleasant evening, and the Burches told strange, beautiful, marvelous things! The two smaller children sang together, and Rebecca, at the request of Mrs. Burch, seated herself at the tinkling old piano and played "Wild roved an Indian girl, bright Alfarata" with considerable spirit and style.

At eight o'clock she crossed the room, handed a palm leaf fan to her Aunt Miranda, ostensibly that she might shade her eyes from the lamplight, but it was a piece of strategy that gave her an opportunity to whisper, "How about cookies?"

"Do you think it's worthwhile?" quavered Miss Miranda in answer.

"The Perkinses always do."

"All right. You know where they be."

Rebecca moved quietly toward the door, and the young Burches followed after her as if they could not bear a second's separation. In five minutes they returned, the little ones bearing plates of thin caraway wafers—hearts, diamonds, and circles daintily sugared and flecked with caraway seed raised in the garden behind the house. These were a specialty of Miss Jane's, and Rebecca carried a tray with cups of tea for the adults—herself included—and milk for the children.

As soon as these refreshments had been genteelly partaken of, Rebecca looked at the clock, rose from her chair in the children's corner, and said cheerfully, "Come! Time for little missionaries to be in bed!"

Everybody laughed at this, the big missionaries most of all, as the young people shook the adults' hands, then disappeared upstairs with Rebecca.

"That niece of yours is the most remarkable girl I have seen in years," said Mr. Burch when the door closed.

"She seems to be turnin' out smart enough lately, but she's consid'able heedless," answered Miranda, "an' much too lively."

"She'd make a wonderful missionary," said Mrs. Burch, "with her voice, and her magnetism, and her gift of language."

"If I was to say which of the two she was best adapted for, I'd say she'd make a better heathen," remarked Miranda curtly.

"My sister don't believe in flattering children," hastily interpolated Jane, glancing toward Mrs. Burch, who seemed somewhat shocked.

Deacon Milliken turned to Miss Sawyer. "Miranda, do you know who Rebecca reminds me of?"

"I can guess pretty well," she replied.

"Then you've noticed it too! I thought at first, seein' she favored her father so on the outside, that she was the same all through. But she ain't, she's like your father, Is--rael Sawyer."

"I don't see how you make that out," said Miranda, thoroughly astonished.

"It struck me this afternoon when she got up to give your invitation in meetin'. It was kind o' curious, but she set in the same seat he used to when he was superintendent of the Sunday school. You know his old way of holding his chin up and throwin' his head back a leetle when he got up to say anything? Well, she done the very same thing. There was more'n one spoke of it."

&a.   &a.   &a.

Rebecca waked before six the next morning, so full of household cares that sleep was impossible. She went to the window and looked out. It was still dark, and a blustering, boisterous day.

"Aunt Jane told me she would get up at half past six and have breakfast at half past seven," she thought. "But I dare say they are both still sick with their colds, and Aunt Miranda will be fidgety with so many in the house. I believe I'll creep down and start things for a surprise."

She put on a corduroy robe and slippers and stole quietly down the tabooed carpeted front stairs, carefully closed the kitchen door behind her so that no noise should waken the rest of the household, busied herself for a half hour with the early morning routine she knew so well, and then went back to her room to dress before calling the children.

Contrary to expectation, Miss Jane, who the evening before felt better than Miranda, grew worse in the night, and was wholly unable to leave her bed in the morning. Miranda grumbled without ceasing during the process of dressing herself, blaming everybody in the universe for the afflictions she had borne and was to bear during the day. She even complained about the Missionary Board that had sent the Burches to Africa, and gave it as her unbiased opinion that those who went to foreign lands for the purpose of saving heathen should stay there and save 'em, and not go gallivantin' all over the earth with a passel o' children, visitin' folks that didn't want 'em and never asked 'em.

Jane lay anxiously and restlessly in bed with a feverish headache, wondering how her sister could manage without her.

Miranda walked stiffly through the dining room, tying a shawl over her head to keep the drafts away, intending to start the breakfast fire and then call Rebecca down, set her to work, and tell her, meanwhile, a few plain facts concerning the proper way of representing the family at a missionary meeting.

She opened the kitchen door and stared vaguely about her, wondering whether she had strayed into the wrong house by mistake.

The shades were up, and there was a crackling fire in the stove. The teakettle was singing and bubbling as it sent out a cloud of steam, and pushed over its nose was a half sheet of note paper with "Compliments of Rebecca" scrawled on it. The coffee pot was scalding, the coffee was measured out in a bowl, and broken eggshells for the settling process were standing near. The cold potatoes and corned beef were in the wooden tray, and "Regards of Rebecca" stuck on the chopping knife. The brown loaf was out, the white loaf was out, the toast rack was out, the doughnuts were out, the milk was skimmed of its cream, the butter had been brought up from the cellar.

Miranda removed the shawl from her head and sank into the kitchen rocker, sputtering under her breath, "She's the beatin'est child! I declare she's all Sawyer!"

ð ð ð

The day and the evening passed off with credit and honor to everybody concerned, even to Jane, who had the discretion to recover instead of growing worse and acting as a damper to the general enjoyment. As the Burches left, the little missionaries, bathed in tears, swore eternal friendship with Rebecca, who pressed into their hands at parting a poem composed before breakfast.

"She's the beatin'est child! I declare she's all Sawyer!"

To Mary and Martha Burch

Born under African skies,
'Neath hotter suns than ours,
The children grew and bloomed,
Like little tropic flowers.

When they first saw the light
'Twas in a heathen land,
Not Greenland's icy mountains,
Nor India's coral strand,

But some mysterious country
Where men are very black
Where of the gospel message
There is a painful lack.

Then let us haste in helping
The Missionary Board
Seek dark-skinned unbelievers,
And teach them of their Lord.

Rebecca Rowena Randall

This visit of the returned missionaries to Riverboro had some far-reaching results. Mr. and Mrs. Burch themselves looked back upon it as one of the rarest pleasures of their year at home. The neighborhood extracted considerable eager conversation from it. Deacon Milliken gave a hundred dollars toward the conversion of Africa, and Mrs. Milliken had a spell of sickness over her husband's rash generosity.

It would be pleasant to state that Miranda Sawyer was an entirely changed woman afterward, but that is not the fact. The tree that has been getting a bad twist for thirty years cannot be straightened in the twinkling of an eye. She became, however, less censorious in her treatment of Rebecca and less harsh in her judgments. Rebecca, Mi-

randa decided after all, had inherited something from the
Sawyer side of the house instead of belonging, mind,
body, and soul, to the despised Randall stock. Everything
that was interesting in Rebecca, and every evidence of
power, capability, or talent afterward displayed by her, Miranda ascribed to the brick house training, and this gave
her a feeling of pride, the pride of a master workman who
has built success out of the most unpromising material.

The brick house did not speedily become a sort of way-
side inn, a place of innocent revelry and joyous welcome.
But the missionary company was an entering wedge, and
Miranda allowed one spare bed to be kept made up "in case
anything should happen," while the company teacups were
kept on the second from the top, instead of the top shelf, in
the china closet. Rebecca had had to stand on a chair to
reach them. Now she could do it by stretching, and this was
symbolic of the way in which she unconsciously scaled the
walls of Miss Miranda's prejudice.

Miranda went so far as to say that she wouldn't mind
if the Burches came every once in a while, but she was
afraid he'd spread abroad the fact of his visit, and
missionaries' families would be underfoot the whole continual time. As a case in point, she gracefully cited the fact
that if a tramp got a good meal at anybody's back door,
'twas said that he'd leave some kind of a sign so that all
the other tramps would know where they were likely to
receive the same treatment.

The effect of the Burches' visit on Rebecca is not so
easily described. Nevertheless, as she looked back upon it
from the vantage ground of after years, she felt that the
moment when she invited the Burches to stay at the brick
house marked an epoch in her life.

18

DAUGHTERS OF ZION

A bijah Flagg was driving over to Wareham on an errand for old Squire Bean, whose general chore boy and farmer's assistant he had been for some years. He passed Emma Jane Perkins' house slowly, as he always did. She was only a girl of fourteen and he a boy of sixteen, but somehow for no particular reason he liked to see the sun shine on her thick braids of reddish-brown hair. He admired her china-blue eyes, too, and her amiable, friendly expression.

Abijah was quite alone in the world, and he always thought that if he had anybody belonging to him he would rather have a sister like Emma Jane Perkins than anything else within the power of the Lord to bestow. When she herself suggested this relationship a few years later, he cast it aside with scorn, having changed his mind in the interval. But that story belongs to another time and place.

Emma Jane was not to be seen in garden, field, or at the window, and Abijah turned his gaze to the large brick house just across the bridge and on the other side of the quiet village street. It might have been closed for a funeral. Neither Miss Miranda nor Miss Jane Sawyer sat at their respective windows knitting, nor was Rebecca Randall's gypsy face to be seen. Ordinarily that will-o-the-wispish little person could be seen, heard, or felt wherever she was.

"The village must be abed," mused Abijah as he neared the Robinsons' yellow cottage, where all the blinds were closed and no sign of life showed on porch or in shed. *No, 'tain't, neither,* he thought again as his horse crept cautiously down the hill, for from the direction of the Robinsons' barn chamber there floated out into the air girlish voices joined in chorus. The words, to a lad brought up in church, were quite recognizable:

> Daughter of Zion, from the dust,
> Exalt thy fallen head!

Abijah pulled up his horse and waited till he caught another familiar verse, beginning:

> Rebuild thy walls, thy bounds enlarge,
> And send thine heralds forth.

"That's Rebecca carrying the melody, and I can hear Emma Jane's alto."

> Say to the North
> Give up thy charge,
> And hold not back, O South,
> And hold not back, O South.

"Land! ain't they smart, seesawin' up an' down in that part they learnt in singin' school! I wonder what they're actin' out, singin' hymn tunes up in the barn chamber? Some o' Becky's doin's, I'll be bound! Git dap, Aleck!"

Aleck pursued his serene and steady trot up the hills along the Saco River, till at length he approached the green Common where the old Tory Hill Meeting House stood, its white paint and green blinds showing fair and pleasant in the afternoon sun. Both doors were open, and

as Abijah turned into the Wareham Road, the church's
pump organ pealed out the opening bars of Heber's "Missionary Hymn," set to Mason's well-known tune, and presently a score of voices sent the good old song from the
choir loft out to the dusty road:

> Shall we whose souls are lighted
> With wisdom from on high,
> Shall we to men benighted
> The lamp of life deny?
> Salvation! O Salvation!
> The joyful sound proclaim,
> Till earth's remotest nation
> Has learned Messiah's name.

"Land!" exclaimed Abijah under his breath. "They're
singin' up here, too! That explains it all. There's a ladies'
missionary meeting at the church, and the girls decided
to hold one o' their own, and I bet ye it's the liveliest of
the two."

The romance of the visit of Mr. and Mrs. Burch, returned missionaries from Africa, had never died in
Rebecca's heart despite the passing of years. And among
the many careers that dazzled her youthful vision was that
of converting the heathen from idol worship to serve
Christ. She thought that by age eighteen she might be suit-
ably equipped for storming some minor citadel of
Mohammedanism. And Mrs. Burch had encouraged her in
the idea because her gift of language, her tact and Christian sympathy, and her musical talent seemed to fit her for
the work.

The quarterly meeting of the Maine Missionary Society
had been set just at the time when a letter from Mrs.
Burch to Miss Jane Sawyer suggested that Rebecca should
form a youth branch in Riverboro. The girls chose an af-

ternoon when every house in the village was vacant and seized the Robinsons' barn hayloft as the place of the meeting.

Rebecca, Alice Robinson, Emma Jane Perkins, Candace Milliken, and Persis Watson, each with her Bible and hymnbook, had climbed the ladder leading to the loft a half-hour before Abijah Flagg had heard the strains of "Daughter of Zion" floating out to the road. Rebecca, being an executive person, had carried, besides her hymnbook, a silver call bell and pencil and paper. An animated discussion regarding one of two names for the society, The Junior Heralds or the Daughters of Zion, had resulted in a unanimous vote for the latter, and Rebecca had been elected president at an early stage of the meeting. She had modestly suggested that Alice Robinson, as the granddaughter of a missionary to China, would be more eligible.

"No," said Alice, with entire good nature, "whoever is *elected* president, you *will* be, Rebecca — you're that kind — so you might as well have the honor. I'd just as soon be secretary, anyway."

"If you should want me to be treasurer, I could be, as well as not," Persis Watson suggested. "For you know, my father keeps china banks at his store — ones that will hold as much as two dollars if you will let them. I think he'd give us one if I happen to be treasurer."

The three principal officers were thus elected at one fell swoop, and with an entire absence of that red tape which commonly renders organization so tiresome, Candace Milliken suggesting that perhaps she'd better be vice-president, as Emma Jane Perkins was always so bashful.

"We ought to have more members," she reminded the other girls, "but if we had invited them the first day they'd have all wanted to be officers, so it's just as well not to ask them till another time. Is Thirza Meserve too little to join?"

"I can't think who anybody named Meserve should have called a baby Thirza," joked Rebecca, somewhat out of order, though the meeting was carried on with small recognition of parliamentary laws. "It always makes me want to say:

> Thirza Meserver,
> Heaven preserve her!

or

> Thirza Meserver,
> Do we deserve her?

She's little, but she's sweet, and absolutely without guile. I think we ought to have her."

"Is *guile* the same as guilt?" inquired Emma Jane Perkins.

"Yes," the president answered knowingly. "Exactly the same, except one is written and the other spoken language. Written language is for poems and graduations and occasions like this — kind of like a best, Sunday-go-to-meeting dress that you wouldn't like to go blueberrying in for fear of getting it spotted."

"I'd just as soon get *guile* spotted as not," flatly affirmed Emma Jane. "I think it's an awful foolish word. But now we're all named and our officers elected, what do we do first? It's easy enough for Mary and Martha Burch. They just play at missionarying because their folks work at it, same as Ted and I used to make believe we were blacksmiths when we were little."

"It must be nicer missionarying in those foreign places," said Persis, "because on 'Afric's shores and India's plains and other spots where Satan reigns' — that's father's favorite hymn — there's always a heathen bowing down to wood and stone. You can take away his idols if he'll let you and give him a Bible, and the beginning's all made. But who'll we begin on? Jethro Small?"

"Oh, he's entirely too dirty, and foolish besides!" exclaimed Candace. "Why not Ethan Hunt? He swears dreadfully."

"He lives on nuts and is a hermit, and it's a mile to his camp through the thick woods. My mother'll never let me go there," objected Alice. "There's Uncle Tut Judson."

"He's too old. He's 'most a hundred and deaf as a post," complained Emma Jane. "Besides, his married daughter is a Sunday school teacher. Why doesn't she teach him to behave? I can't think of anybody just right to start on!"

"Don't talk like that, Emma Jane," Rebecca's tone had a tinge of reproof in it. "We are a missionary body named the Daughters of Zion, and, of course, we've got to find something to do."

"I can't for the life of me see how you can help being a heathen if you're born in Africa," persisted Persis, who was well named.

"You can't." Rebecca was clear on this point. "I had that all out with Mrs. Burch when she was visiting Aunt Miranda. She says they can't help being heathen, but all the same, they're accountable to God for their sins. It's our job to tell them the gospel and get them saved."

"Are there plenty of stagecoaches and railroads in Africa?" asked Alice. "Because there must be dreadfully long distances, and what if missionaries couldn't pay the fare?"

"That's why we will save our pennies and nickels and dimes for the missionaries," explained Rebecca. "Our job here in America is to raise money to send them to the heathen."

"I think it's awful rude, anyway, to go right out and try to convert your neighbors," said Emma Jane uncertainly. "But if you borrow a horse and go to North Riverboro or Milliken's Mills I s'pose that makes it foreign missions."

"Would we each go alone or wait upon them with a committee, as they did when they asked Deacon Tuttle for a contribution for the new hearse?" asked Persis.

"Oh! we must go alone," decided Rebecca. "It would be much more refined and delicate. Aunt Miranda says that one man alone could never get a subscription from Deacon Tuttle, and that's the reason they sent a committee. Now let's all think quietly for a minute or two who's the very most heathenish and reperrehensiblest person in Riverboro."

After a very brief period of silence, the words *Jacob Moody* fell from all lips with entire accord.

"You are right," said the president tersely. "And after singing hymn number two hundred seventy-four, to be found on the sixty-sixth page, we will take up the question of persuading Mr. Moody to attend church or the minister's Bible class, he not having been in the church meeting house for lo! these many years:

> Daughter of Zion, the power that hath
> saved thee
> Extolled with the harp and the timbrel
> should be.

"Sing without reading, if you please, omitting the second stanza. Hymn two-seventy-four, to be found on the sixty-sixth page of the new hymnbook or on page thirty-two of Emma Jane Perkins's old one."

19

A MISSIONARY JOURNEY

I t is doubtful if Mr. Burch had ever found in Africa a person more difficult to persuade than the already gospel-hardened Jacob Moody of Riverboro. Tall, gaunt, swarthy, black-bearded—his masses of grizzled, uncombed hair and the red scar across his nose and cheek added to his sinister appearance. His tumbledown house stood on a rocky bit of land back of the old Sawyer pasture, and the acres of his farm stretched out on all sides of it. He lived alone, ate alone, plowed, planted, sowed, and harvested alone. And everybody believed he would die alone as "unwept, unhonored, and unsung" as the man without a country.

The road that bordered his fields was comparatively little used by anyone, and although it was thickly set with chokecherry trees and blackberry bushes, it had been for years practically deserted even by the children on berry-picking trips. Jacob's Wolf River and Granny Garland trees hung thick with apples, but no Riverboro boy stole them, for terrifying accounts of the fate that had overtaken one urchin in times gone by had been handed along from boy to boy, protecting the Moody fruit far better than any police patrol.

This then was the person whose moral and spiritual re-habilitation was to be accomplished by the Daughters of Zion. But how?

"Who will volunteer to visit Mr. Moody?" asked President Rebecca.

"Nobody'll volunteer, Rebecca Rowena Randall, and you know it," said Emma Jane.

"Why don't we draw lots, when none of us wants to speak to him, and yet one of us must?"

This suggestion fell from Persis Watson, who had been pale and thoughtful ever since the first mention of Jacob Moody.

"Wouldn't it be wicked to settle it that way?"

"It's gamblers that draw lots."

"People did it in the Bible ever so often."

"It doesn't seem nice for a missionary meeting."

These remarks fell all together upon the president's be-wildered ear while she was trying to adjust this difficult dilemma.

"It is a very puzzly question," she said thoughtfully. "I could ask Aunt Jane if we had time, but I suppose we haven't. It doesn't seem nice to draw lots, and yet how can we settle it without? We know we mean right, and perhaps it will be right. Alice, take this paper and tear off five narrow pieces, all different lengths."

At this moment a voice from a distance floated up to the hayloft—a voice saying plaintively: "Will you let me play with you, girls? Huldah has gone to ride, and I'm all alone."

It was the voice of the absolutely-without-guile little Thirza Meserve, and it came at an opportune moment.

"If she is going to be a member," said Persis, "why not let her come up and hold the lots? She'd be real honest and not favor anybody."

It seemed an excellent idea, and it was followed up so quickly that scarcely three minutes passed before the guileless one was holding the five scraps in her hot little palm, laboriously changing their places again and again until they looked exactly alike and all rather soiled and wilted. "Come, girls, draw!" commanded the president. "Thirza, you mustn't chew gum at a missionary meeting. It isn't polite nor holy. Take it out and stick it somewhere till the exercises are over."

The five Daughters of Zion approached the spot so charged with fate and extended their trembling hands one by one. Then after a moment's silent clutching of their papers, they drew nearer to one another and compared them.

Emma Jane Perkins had drawn the short one, becoming thus the chosen instrument for Jacob Moody's conversion! She looked about her despairingly, as if to seek some painless and respectable method of self-destruction. "Do let's draw over again," she pleaded. "I'm the worst of all of us. I'm sure to make a mess of it till I kind o' get trained in."

Rebecca's heart sank at this frank confession, which only corroborated her own fears. "I'm sorry, Emmy, dear," she said, "but our only excuse for drawing lots at all would be to have it sacred. We must think of it as a kind of a sign, almost like God speaking to Moses in the burning bush."

"Oh, I *wish* there was a burning bush right here!" cried the distracted and reluctant missionary. "How quick I'd step into it without even stopping to take off my garnet ring!"

"Don't be such a scaredy cat, Emma Jane!" exclaimed Candace bracingly. "Jacob Moody can't kill you, even if he has an awful temper. Trot right along now before you get more frightened. Shall we go with her, Rebecca, and wait at the pasture gate? Then whatever happens, Alice can put it down in the minutes of the meeting."

In these terrible crises of life time gallops with such incredible velocity that it seemed to Emma Jane only a breath before she was being dragged through the fields by the Daughters of Zion, the guileless little Thirza panting in the rear.

At the gate to the pasture Rebecca gave Emma an impassioned embrace, and whispering, *"Whatever you do, be careful how you lead up,"* lifted off the top rail and pushed her over the bars. Then the girls each sought a tree under whose friendly protection she could watch, and perhaps pray, until the missionary should return from her field of labor. Rebecca herself, as president of the society, dutifully scrambled to the topmost branches of an ancient apple tree by the pasture gate, from where, if she could not help Emma, she could at least pray with knowledge.

Alice Robinson, whose compositions were always marked 96 or 97 (100 symbolizing such perfection as could not be attained in the mortal world of Riverboro), Alice, not only Daughter, but Scribe of Zion, sharpened her pencil with her penknife and wrote a few well-chosen words of introduction, to be used when the records of the afternoon had been made by Emma Jane Perkins and Jacob Moody.

Rebecca's heart beat tumultuously under her gingham dress as she clung to the tree. She felt that a drama was being enacted, and though unfortunately she was not the central figure, she had at least a modest part in it. The short lot had not fallen to the most able Daughter; that she quite realized. Yet would any one of them succeed in winning Jacob Moody's attention, in engaging him in pleasant conversation, and finally in bringing him to a realization of his mistaken way of life and converting him, or at least getting him to agree to attend church? She doubted, but at the same moment her spirits rose at the thought of the difficulties involved in the undertaking.

Difficulties always spurred Rebecca on, but they daunted poor Emma Jane, who had no little thrills of excitement and wonder and fear and longing to sustain her lagging soul. That her attempt at witnessing was to be entered as "minutes" by a secretary seemed to her the last straw. Her blue eyes looked lighter than usual and had the glaze of china saucers. Her usually pink cheeks were pale, but she pressed on, determined to be a faithful Daughter of Zion, and above all to be worthy of Rebecca's admiration and respect.

Rebecca can do anything, she thought, with enthusiastic loyalty, *and I mustn't be any stupider than I can help, or she'll choose one of the other girls for her most intimate friend.* So, mustering all her courage, she turned into Jacob Moody's dooryard where he was splitting his winter firewood.

"It's a pleasant afternoon, Mr. Moody," she said in a polite but hoarse whisper. Rebecca's words, *Lead up! Lead up!* rang in clarion tones through her brain.

Jacob Moody looked at her curiously. "Good enough, I guess," he growled. "But I don't never have time to look at afternoons."

Emma Jane seated herself timidly on the end of a large log near the chopping block hoping that Jacob, like other hosts, would pause in his tasks and chat. She was, in fact, relieved and somewhat surprised that the old man did not chase her off with his ax.

The block is kind of like an idol, she thought. *I wish I could take it away from him, and then perhaps he'd talk.*

At this moment Jacob raised his ax and came down on the block with such a stunning blow that Emma Jane fairly leaped into the air.

"You'd better look out, Sissy, or you'll git chips in the eye!" said Moody, grimly going on with his work. His voice, though matter-of-fact, was not angry at least.

The Daughter of Zion sent up a silent prayer for inspiration, but none came, and she sat silent, giving nervous jumps in spite of herself whenever the ax fell upon the log Jacob was splitting.

Finally the host became tired of his speechless visitor. Leaning on his ax, he said, "Look here, Sis, what have you come for? What's you errant? Do you want apples? Or cider? Or what? Speak out or git out, one or t' other."

Emma Jane, who had wrung her handkerchief into a clammy ball, gave it a last despairing wrench and faltered, "Wouldn't you like. . . hadn't you better. . . don't you think you'd ought to attend church and Sunday school? I'm sure Father would pick you up in his wagon come Sunday mornin'," she went on politely, her voice by now a mouselike squeak.

Jacob's ax almost dropped from his nerveless hand, and he regarded the Daughter of Zion with unspeakable rage and disdain. Then, the blood mounting in his face, he gathered himself together and shouted, "You take yourself off that log and out o' this dooryard double quick, you impudent, sanct'omus young one! You just let me ketch Bill Perkins's child trying to teach me where I shall go, at my age! Scuttle, I tell ye! And if I see your ugly little mug inside my fence again, I'll chase ye down the hill or set the dog on ye! *Scoot, I tell ye!*"

Emma Jane obeyed orders summarily, taking herself off the log, out the dooryard, and scuttling and scooting down the hill at a pace never imagined even by Jacob

"You take yourself off that log and out o' this dooryard double quick."

Moody, who stood regarding her flying heels with a sardonic grin. Down she stumbled, the tears coursing over her cheeks and mingling with the dust of her flight, till with a hysterical shriek she fell over the bars and into Rebecca's arms outstretched to receive her. The other Daughters wiped her eyes and supported her, while Thirza, thoroughly frightened, burst into sympathetic tears.

No questions were asked, for it was felt by all that Emma Jane's demeanor answered them before they could be uttered.

"He threatened to set the dog on me!" she wailed presently, as they neared the Sawyer pasture. "He said he'd chase me out o' the dooryard if I ever came again! And he'll tell my father — I know he will."

All at once the adult point of view dawned upon Rebecca. She never saw it until it was too obvious to be ignored. Had they done wrong in trying to convert Jacob Moody? Would Aunt Miranda be angry, as well as Mr. Perkins?

"Why was he so dreadful, Emmy?" she questioned tenderly. "What did you say first? How did you lead up to it?"

Emma Jane sobbed more convulsively, and she wiped her nose and eyes frantically as she tried to think. "I guess I never led up at all, not a mite. I didn't know what you meant. I was sent on an errant, and I went and done it the best I could! And then Jake roared at me like Squire Bean's bull. And he called my face an ugly mug. You shut up that secretary book, Alice Robinson! If you write down a single word, I'll never speak to you again. And I don't want to be a member another minute for fear of drawing another short lot. I've had enough of the Daughters of Zion to last me the rest o' my life! I don't care who goes to church and who don't."

The girls were at the Perkins' gate by this time, and Emma Jane went sadly into the empty house to remove all traces of the tragedy from her face and clothes before her mother came home from church. The others wended their way slowly down the street, feeling that their promising missionary branch had died almost as soon as it had budded.

"Good-by," said Rebecca, swallowing lumps of disappointment and chagrin as she saw the whole inspiring plan break and vanish into thin air like an iridescent bubble. "Aunt Jane must write Mrs. Burch that we don't want to be home missionaries. Perhaps we're not old enough, anyway. I'm perfectly certain it's nicer to convert people when they're yellow or brown or any color but white. And I believe it must be easier to save their souls than it is to make them go to church."

   èà èà èà

As things turned out, old Jake Moody did not tell Mr. Perkins about Emma Jane's attempt to convert him. The Sunday following, Rebecca, who was walking home from church with Aunt Jane — Aunt Miranda having stayed abed with a sick headache — mentioned to her aunt that Mrs. Burch must be told that there would be no youth missionary society in Riverboro.

"Why not, Becky?" inquired the unsuspecting aunt.

Rebecca related the episode at Jacob Moody's place in all its frightening detail. "Do you suppose the Burches get treated like that in Africa, Aunty?" Rebecca concluded.

"I'm sure it happens, dear," Aunt Jane answered. "But I'm sure if we began our witnessin' by bein' kind and generous to folks more like ourselves, witnessin' to . . . to heathen like Mr. Moody would come easier, when the Lord gives us opportunity."

"Oh." Rebecca was thoughtful a long moment. "I guess I could start by bein' nice to Minnie Smellie *all* the time. And by loving even Aunt Miranda."

"Even Aunt Miranda," Jane repeated softly, dabbing a tear from the corner of her eye.

20

REBECCA'S SECRET CHAMBER

T he barn, which was attached to the brick house by a long ell or shed, still had its haymow in Rebecca's time, although the hay was a dozen years old or more, and in the opinion of the occasional visiting horse, sadly juiceless and wanting in flavor. It still sheltered, too, old Deacon Israel Sawyer's carryall wagon and mowing machine, as well as the pung with which he'd hauled many a load of firewood for the winter, his sleigh, and a dozen other survivals of an earlier era, when the broad acres of the brick house went to make one of the finest farms in the valley of the Saco.

There were no horses or cows in the stalls nowadays; no pig grunted comfortably of future spareribs and pork chops in the sty. Only the hens, kept in an old horse stall in the barn, were left to peck the plants in the cherished garden patch. The Misses Jane and Miranda Sawyer were not of a mind to walk outdoors to the backyard henhouse in winter.

The Sawyer girls were getting on in years, and mindful that care once killed a cat, they ordered their lives with the

view of escaping that particular doom, at least, and succeeded fairly well until Rebecca's coming made existence
a trifle more sensational. Once a month for years and years
Miss Miranda and Miss Jane had put towels over their
heads and made a solemn visit to the barn, taking off the
enameled cloth coverings, dusting the ancient implements,
and sometimes sweeping the heaviest of the cobwebs from
the corners or giving a brush to the chaffy floor.

Deacon Israel's tottering ladder still stood in its accustomed place, propped against the haymow, and the heavenly stairway leading to eternal glory scarcely looked
fairer to Jacob of old than this did to Rebecca. By means
of its worn, wobbly rounds she mounted, mounted,
mounted far away from childish tasks and childish troubles, to a hidden chamber. This was a place so full of
golden dreams, happy reveries, and vague longings, that as
her little brown hands clung to the sides of the ladder and
her feet trod the rounds cautiously in her climb, her heart
almost stopped beating in the sheer joy of anticipation.

Once having gained the heights through a trapdoor in
the chamber floor, her next move was to unlatch a heavy
upper door and give it a gentle swing outward. Then, oh
ever-new paradise! Then, oh ever lovely green and growing
world! For Rebecca had that something in her soul that,

> Gives to seas and sunset skies
> The unspent beauty of surprise.

At the top of Guide Board Hill, Rebecca could see
Alice Robinson's barn with its shining weathervane, a
huge burnished copper fish that glowed in the sun and
swam with the wind to foretell the day to all Riverboro.
The meadow behind the brick house, with its sunny slopes
stretching to the river, was sometimes a flowing sheet of
shimmering grass, sometimes—when daisies and butter-

cups were blooming—a vision of white and gold. Sometimes the shorn stubble would be dotted with happy hills
of hay stacked into cocks by Alice Robinson's father, who
paid Miranda Sawyer for it with a side of beef each fall. In
autumn, the rock maples among the pines along the river
would stand out like golden balls against the green, the
sugar maples among them glowing brave in scarlet.

It was on one of these autumn days with a wintry nip in
the air that Adam Ladd, Rebecca's favorite "Mr. Aladdin,"
after searching for her in field and garden, suddenly noticed
the open door of the barn chamber swung wide, high up in
the gable end facing the fields. He called to her, and at the
sound of his voice she dropped her precious diary and flew
to the edge of the chamber. Adam never forgot the vision of
the startled, slender young poetess, book in one mittened
hand, pencil in the other, dark hair all ruffled, with the pic-
turesque addition of an occasional blade of straw, her
cheeks crimson, her eyes shining.

"A Sappho in mittens!" he cried laughingly, and at her
eager question told her to look up the unknown lady in the
high school encyclopedia when she entered Wareham
Academy next fall. His errand that day had been to deliver
a letter from his aunt to the Misses Sawyer. So leaving the
missive at their door, he went on his way without making
their acquaintance.

Now all being ready, Rebecca went to a corner of the
room and withdrew a thick, blank book of ruled pages and
mottled covers from behind a loose board. Out of her
gingham apron pocket came a pencil and an eraser. Then
she seated herself gravely on the floor and drew an in-
verted wooden soapbox nearer to her for a table.

The book was reverently opened, and there was a serious reading of the extracts already carefully written in it.
Most of them were apparently to the writer's liking, for

dimples of pleasure showed themselves now and then, and smiles of obvious delight played about her face. But once in a while there was a knitting of the brows and a sigh of discouragement, showing that the artistic nature in the girl was not wholly satisfied.

Then came the crucial moment when the budding author was supposed to be racked with the throes of composition, but seemingly there were no throes. Other girls could wield the darning or crochet or knitting needle, and send the tatting shuttle through loops of the finest cotton. They could hemstitch, oversew, and braid hair in thirteen strands. But the pencil was never obedient to their fingers, and the pen and inkwell were to most of them a horror from early childhood to the end of time.

Not so with Rebecca. Her pencil moved as easily as her tongue, and her tongue could move like a well-oiled sewing machine bobbin when its mistress would permit it. Her handwriting was not Spencerian, with its calligraphic flourishes and practiced slants of exactly fifty-two degrees. She had neither time nor patience, it is to be feared, for copybook methods. And her formless characters were frequently the despair of her teachers. But write she could, write she would, write she must and did, in season and out. From the time she first lifted a pen at six till now, writing was the easiest of all possible tasks, to be indulged in as solace and balm when the mathematical terrors of examples in least common multiples threatened to dethrone the reason, or the rules of grammar and diagrammed sentences loomed huge and unconquerable in her near horizon.

As to spelling, it came to her in the main by free grace and not by training. And though she slipped at times from the beaten path, her extraordinary ear and good visual memory kept her from many or flagrant mistakes. It was her intention, especially when saying her prayers at night, to look up all doubtful words in her small leather-bound dictionary before copying her thoughts into her sacred book for the inspiration of posterity. But when genius burned with a brilliant flame, and particularly when she was in the barn and the dictionary in the house, impulse as usual carried the day.

There sits Rebecca, then, pencil in hand, Thought Book on her soap box desk, in the open door of the Sawyer's barn chamber — the sunset door. How many a time had her grandfather, the good deacon, sat just underneath this same door in his tipped-back chair. But the deacon, looking on his waving grass fields, his tasseling corn, and his timberlands, bright and honest as were his eyes, never saw such visions as Rebecca saw. The girl, transplanted from her home farm at Sunnybrook, from the care of her overworked but easygoing mother and the companionship of the scantily fed, scantily clothed, happy-go-lucky brothers and sisters — she had indeed fallen on pleasant places and shady days in Riverboro.

There sits Rebecca, then, pencil in hand . . .

21

REBECCA'S THOUGHT BOOK

I f you opened the mottled covers of Rebecca's carefully guarded Thought Book, you would first have seen a wonderful title page, constructed apparently on the same lines as the inscription on a tombstone, except for the quantity and variety of information contained in it. Much of the matter would seem to the reader better adapted to the body of the book than to the title page, but Rebecca was anxious that the principal persons in her chronicle should be well described at the outset.

THOUGHT BOOK
of
Rebecca Rowena Randall

Really of
Sunnybrook Farm
But Temporily of
The Brick House in Riverboro.
Own niece of Miss Miranda and Jane Sawyer

Second of seven children of her father, Mr. L. D. M. Randall
(Now at rest under the willow tree at Sunnybrook)
Also of her mother, Mrs. Aurelia Randall.

In case of Death the best of these Thoughts
May be printed in my Remerniscences
For the Sunday School Library at Temperance, Maine
Which needs more books fearfully
And I hereby do Will and Testament them
To Mr. Adam Ladd
Who bought 300 cakes of soap from me
And thus secured a premium
A greatly needed banquet lamp
For my friends the Simpsons.
He is the only one that incourages
My writing Remerniscences and
My teacher Miss Dearborn will
Have much valuable Poetry and Thoughts
To give him unless carelessly destroyed.

The pictures are by the same hand that
Wrote the Thoughts.

*It is not now decided whether Rebecca Rowena Randall
will be a painter or an author, but after her death it will
be known which she has been, if any.*

FINIS

ช   ช   ช

From the title page, with its wealth of detail, the book
ripples on like a brook, and to the weary reader of novels
it may have something of the brook's refreshing qualities.

Our Diaries

May 8

All the girls are keeping a diary because Miss Dearborn was very much ashamed when the school trustees told her that most of the girls' and all of the boys' compositions were disgraceful and must be improved on next term. She asked the boys to write letters to her once a week instead of keeping a diary, which they thought was girlish, like playing with dolls. The boys thought it was dreadful to have to write letters every seven days, but she told them it was not half as bad for them as it was for her who had to read them.

To make my diary a little different, I am going to call it a Thought Book, written just like that, with capitals. I have thoughts that I never can use unless I write them down, for Aunt Miranda always says, "Keep your thoughts to yourself." Aunt Jane lets me tell her some, but does not like my queer ones, and my true ones are mostly queer. Emma Jane does not mind hearing them now and then, and that is my only chance.

If Miss Dearborn does not like the name *Thought Book*, I will call it *Remerniscences*. Remerniscences are thoughts you remember about yourself and write down in case you should die. Aunt Jane doesn't like to read any other kind of books but just lives of interesting dead people, and she says that is what Longfellow, who was born in the state of Maine and we should be very proud of it, meant in his poem:

> Lives of great men all remind us
> We should make our lives sublime,
> And departing, leave behind us
> Footprints in the sands of time.

I know what this means, because when Emma Jane and I went to the beach with Uncle Jerry Cobb we ran along the wet sand and looked at the shapes our boots made, just as if they were stamped in wax. Emma Jane turns in her left foot ("splayfoot," the boys call it, which is not polite), and Seth Strout had just patched one of my shoes, and it all came out in the sand like pictures.

When I learned "The Psalm of Life" for Friday afternoon speaking, I thought I shouldn't like to leave a patched footprint, nor have Emma Jane's print look crooked on the sands of time, and right away I thought, *Oh! what a splendid thought for my Thought Book when Aunt Jane buys me a fifteen-cent one over to Watson's store.*

Remerniscences

June 15

I told Aunt Jane I was going to begin my Remerniscences, and she says I am too young, but I reminded her that Candace Milliken's sister died when she was thirteen, leaving no footprints whatever, and if I should die suddenly, who would write down my Remerniscences? Aunt Miranda says the sun and moon would rise and set just the same, and it was no matter if they didn't get written down, and to go up to the attic and find her piece bag. But I said it would, as there was only one of everybody in the world, and nobody else could do their Remerniscensing for them.

If I should die tonight, I know not who would describe me right. Miss Dearborn would say one thing and brother John another. Emma Jane would try to do me justice, but she has no words. And I am glad Aunt Miranda never takes the pen in hand except to write leters which have no thoughts.

My dictionary is so small it has not many genteel words in it, and I cannot find how to spell Remerniscences, but I remember from the cover of Aunt Jane's book that there was an *s* and a *c* close together in the middle of it, which I thought foolish and not needful.

All the girls like their diaries very much, but Minnie Smellie got Alice Robinson's where she hid it under the school woodpile and read it all through. She said it was no worse than reading anybody's composition, but we told her it was just like peeking through a keyhole, or listening at a window, or opening someone else's bureau drawer. She said she didn't look at it that way, and I told her that unless her eyes got unsealed she would never leave any kind of a sublime footprint on the sands of time. I told her a diary was very sacred, as you generally poured your deepest feelings into it, expecting nobody to look at it but yourself and your indulgent Heavenly Father who seeeth all things.

Of course it would not hurt Persis Watson to show her diary because she has not a sacred plan, and this is the way it goes, for she reads it out loud to us:

Arose at six this morning—(you always arise in a diary, but you say 'get up' when you talk about it). Ate breakfast at half past six. Had soda biscuits, coffee, fish hash and doughnuts. Wiped the dishes, fed the hens and made my bed before school. Had a good arithmetic lesson, but went down two points in spelling. At half past four played hide and coop in the Sawyer pasture. Swept store out for Father, then went to bed at eight.

She says she can't put in what doesn't happen, but as I don't think her diary is interesting, she will ask her mother to have meat hash instead of fish, with pie when the doughnuts give out, and she will feed the hens before breakfast to make a change. We are all going now to try and make something happen every single day, so the diaries won't be so dull and the footprints so common.

An Uncommon Thought

September 12

We dug up our rosecakes today, and that gave me a good Remerniscence. The way you make rosecakes is, you take the leaves of full blown roses and mix them with a little cinnamon and as much brown sugar as your mother (in my case, my aunts) will give you (which is never half enough, except Persis Watson, whose affectionate parents let her go to the barrel in their store). Then you do up little bits like Seidlitz powders, first in soft paper and then in brown, and bury them in the ground and let them stay as long as you possibly can hold out. Then dig them up and eat them.

Emma Jane and I stick up little signs over the holes in the ground with the date we buried them and when they'll be done enough to dig up, but we can never wait. When Aunt Jane saw us, she said it was the first thing for children to learn — not to be impatient. When I went to the barn chamber, I made this poem:

> We dug our rose cakes up, oh all too soon.
> 'Twas in the orchard just at noon.
> 'Twas on a bright July forenoon.
> 'Twas in the sunny afternoon.
> 'Twas underneath the harvest moon.

It was not that way at all. It was a foggy morning before school, and I should think poets could never possibly get to heaven, for it is so hard to stick to the truth when you are writing poetry. Emma Jane thinks it is nobody's business when we dug the rosecakes up. I like the line about the harvest moon best, but it would give a wrong idea of our lives and characters to the people that read my Thoughts, for they would think we were up late nights, so I have fixed it like this:

> We dug our rosecakes up, oh all too soon,
> We thought their sweetness would be such
>   a boon.
> We ne'er suspicioned they could not be
>   done
> After three days of autumn wind and sun.
> Why did we from the earth our treasures
>   draw?
> 'Twas not for fear that rat or mole might
>   naw,
> An aged aunt doth say impatience was the
>   reason,
> She says that youth is ever out of season.

That is just as Aunt Jane said it, and it gave me the thought for the poem which is rather uncommon.

Rewards

October 3

It is hard to find rewards for yourself, but perhaps Aunt Jane and some of the girls would each give me one to help out. I could carry my bead purse to school every day, or wear my silver locket a little while before I go to sleep at night. I could read *Cora, Sorrows of a Doctor's Wife* a little oftener, but that's all the rewards I can think of. I fear Aunt Miranda would say they are wicked. But oh, if they should turn out benefercent, how glad and joyful life would be to me! A sweet and beautiful character, beloved by my teacher and schoolmates, admired and petted by my aunts and neighbors, yet carrying my bead purse constantly with perhaps my best hat on Wednesday afternoons, as well as Sundays!

A Great Shock

October 11

The reason why Alice Robinson could not play was, she was being punished for breaking her mother's best blue willow platter. Just before supper, my story being finished, I went up Guide Board Hill to see how she was bearing up, and she spoke to me from her window. She said she did not mind being punished because she hadn't been for a long time, and she hoped it would help her with her composition. She thought it would give her thoughts, and tomorrow's the last day for her to have any. This gave me a good idea, and I told her to call her father up and beg him to spank her hard. It would hurt, I said, but perhaps none of the other girls would have a punishment like that since girls don't get spanked as often as boys, and her composition would be all different and splendid. If her father used a switch on her legs, I would borrow Aunt Miranda's witch hayzel and pour it on her wounds like the Samaritan in the Bible. Witch hayzel smarts wicked fierce on chapped skin, so Alice could really write about suffering.

I went up again after supper with Dick Carter to see how it turned out. Alice came to the window, and Dick threw up a note tied to a stick. I had written: Demand your punishment to the full. Behave like Delores' mother in "The Martyrs of Spain." She threw down an answer, and it was: You just be Delores' mother yourself if you're so smart. Then she stamped away from the window, and my feelings were hurt, but Dick said perhaps she was hungry, and that made her cross. And as Dick and I turned to go out of the yard, we looked back and saw something I can never forget. (The Great Shock) Mrs. Robinson was out behind the barn feeding the turkies. Mr. Robinson came softly out of the side door in the orcherd, and looking everywheres around, he stepped to the wire cooler closet and took out a saucer of cold beans with a pickled beet on top, and a big piece of blueberry pie. Then he crept up the back stairs, and we could see Alice open her door and take in the supper.

Oh, what will become of her composition, and how can she tell anything on the benefercent effects of punishment, when she is locked up by one parent, and fed by the other? I have forgiven her for the way she snapped at me, for, of course, you couldn't beg your father to spank you when he was bringing you blueberry pie. Mrs. Robinson makes a kind that leeks out a thick purple juice into the plate and needs a spoon and blacks your mouth, but it is heavenly.

A Dream

October 14

The week is almost up, and very soon Dr. Moses will drive up to the schoolhouse like Elijah in the chariot and come in to hear us read. There is a good deal of sickness among us. Some of the boys are not able to come to school just now, but hope to be up and about again by Monday, when Dr. Moses goes away to a convention.

"Rewards and Punishments" is a very hard composition to write, somehow. Last night I dreamed that the river was ink, and I kept dipping into it and writing with a pen made of a young pine tree. I sliced great slabs of marble off the side of one of the White Mountains, the one you see going to church, and wrote on those. Then I threw them all into the falls, not being good enough for Dr. Moses.

Dick Carter had a splendid boy stay over Sunday. He makes the real newspaper named *The Pilot,* published by the students at Wareham Academy. He says when he talks about himself in writing he calls himself "we," and it sounds much more like print besides consealing him more.

Example: Our hair was measured this morning and has grown two inches since last time. . . . Our ink spot that we made by negligence on our only white petticoat we have been able to remove with lemon and milk. Some of our petticoat came out with the spot.

I shall try it in my composition sometime, for, of course, I shall write for *The Pilot* when I go to Wareham. Uncle Jerry Cobb says that I shall, and thinks that in a couple of years I might rise to be editor if they ever have girls.

I have never been more good than since I have been rewarding myself steady, even to asking Aunt Miranda kindly to offer me a company jelly tart, not because I was hungry, but for an experement I was trying, and would explain to her sometime. She said she never thought it was wise to experement with your stomach, and I said, with a queer thrilling look, it was not my stomach but my soul, that was being tried. Then she gave me the tart and walked away all puzzled and nervous.

We had the wrath of God four times in sermons this last summer, but our minister, Mr. Baxter, says that God is love, too, so I guess it is onley fair for God to be angry once in a while.

Mr. Baxter is different and calls his wife "Honey," which is lovely and the first time I ever heard it in Riverboro. Mrs. Baxter is another kind of people, too, from those that live in Temperance. I like to watch her in church and see her listen to her husband who is young and handsome for a minister. That gives me very queer and uncommon fealings, when they look at each other, which they always do when not otherwise engaged. She has different clothes from anybody else. Aunt Miranda says you must onley think of two things: will your dress keep you warm and will it wear well, and there is nobody in the world to know how I love pink and red and how I hate drab and green and how I never wear my hat with the black and yellow porkupine quills without wishing it would blow into the river.

Stories and People

October 21

There are people in books and people in Riverboro, and they are not the same kind. They never talk of chargers and palfreys in the village, nor say "How oft" and "Methinks," and if a Scotchman out of *Rob Roy* should come to Riverboro and want to marry one of us girls, we could not understand him unless he made motions. Though Huldah Meserve says if a nobleman of high degree should ask her to be his—one of vast estates with serfs at his bidding—she would be able to guess his meaning in any language.

Uncle Jerry Cobb thinks that Riverboro people would not make a story, but I know that some of them would.

Mrs. Peter Meserve says Grandpa Sawyer was once a wonderful hand at stories. She says he was the life of the store and barber shop when he was a young man, and she thinks I take after him because I like compositions better than all the other lessons. But Mother says I take after Father, who always could say everything nicely whether he had anything to say or not. So methinks I should be grateful to both of them. They are what is called ancestors, and much depends upon whether you have them or not. Of course, everyone has ancestors, even the Simpsons, but some people's aren't so great.

Aunt Miranda says the reason everybody is so prosperous around here is because their ancestors were all first settlers and raised on burnt ground. This should make us very proud, but not so proud we can't be nice to people like the Simpsons, who have moved a lot.

Methinks and *methought* are splendid words for compositions. Miss Dearborn likes them very much, but Alice and I never bring them in to suit her. *Methought* means the same as I thought, but sounds better. Example: If you are telling a dream you had about your aged aunt:

> Methought I heard her say
> "My child, you have so useful been
> You need not sew today."

This afternoon I was walking over to the store to buy molasses, and as I came off the bridge and turned up the hill, I saw lots and lots of heelprints in the side of the road — heelprints with little spike holes in them.

"The river drivers have come from upcountry," I thought, "and they'll be breaking up the log jam above our falls tomorrow." But I looked everywhere about and not a man did I see, but still I knew I was not mistaken, for heel prints could not lie. All the way over and back I thought about it, though unfortunately forgetting the molasses, and Alice Robinson not being able to come out, I took playtime to write a story. It is the first grown-up one I ever did and is intended to be like *Cora, the Doctor's Wife*, not a school composition. It is written for Mr. Adam Ladd, and people like him who live in Boston, and is the printed kind you get money for to pay off a morgage.

Lancelot or the Parted Lovers

November 9

A beautiful village maiden was betrothed to a stalwart French Canadien river driver, but they had high and bitter words and parted, he to weep in the crystal stream where he drove his logs, and she to sigh and moan as she went about her round of household tasks.

At eventide the maiden went to lean over the bridge, and her tears fell into the foaming stream. So, though the two unhappy lovers did not know it, the river was their friend, the only one to whom they told their secrets and wept into.

The months crept on, and it was the next July when the maiden was passing over the bridge and up the hill. Suddenly she spied footprints on the sands of time.

"The river drivers have come again!" she cried, putting her hand to her breast, for she had a slight heart trouble like Cora and Mrs. Meserve, that doesn't kill.

"They have come indeed, *especially* one you knew," said a voice, and out of the alder bushes sprang Lancelot Ladd, for that was the lover's name, and it was none other than he. His hair was curly and like living gold. His shirt, while of flannel, was new and dry, and of a handsome red color, and as the maiden looked at him she could think of nought but a fairy prince.

"Forgive me," she mermered, stretching out her waisted hands.

"Nay, Sweet," he replied, "Tis I that should say that to you," and bending gracefully on one knee he kissed the hem of her dress. It was a rich pink gingham check, elaborately ornamented with white tape trimming.

Clasping each other to the heart like Cora and the doctor, they stood there for a long while till they heard the rumble of wheels on the bridge and knew they must disentangle.

The wheels came nearer and nearer, and verily it was the maiden's father.

"Can I wed your fair daughter this very moon?" asked Lancelot, who will not be called his whole name again in this story.

"You may," said the father, "for lo, she has been ready and waiting for many months." This he said, not knowing how he was shaming the maiden, whose name was Linda Rowenetta.

Then and there the nuptial day was appointed, and when it came, the marriage knot was tied upon the river bank where first they met, the river bank where they had parted in anger and where they had again sealed their vows and clasped each other to the heart. And it was very low water that summer, and the river always thought it was because the tears dropped into it had stopped, but there were so many smiles that the sunshine dried it up.

R. R. R.

FINIS

Our Secret Society

November 16

Our Secret Society has just had a splendid picnic in Candace Milliken's barn. Our name is the BOSS, and not a single boy in the village has been able to guess it. Some said that girls are BOSSy, or it might be for BOSSy cow, but that is mean.

It means Braid Over Shoulder Society, and that is our sign. All of the members wear one of their braids over their right shoulder in front. The president's tied with a red ribbon (I am the president), and all the rest are tied with blue.

To attract the attention of another member when in company or at a public place, we take the braid between the thumb and little finger and stand carelessly on one leg. This is the Secret Signal and the password is Ssob (BOSS spelled backwards) which was my idea and is thought rather uncommon.

One of the rules of the BOSS is that any member may be required to tell her besetting sin at any meeting if asked to do so by a majority of the members. This was Candace Milliken's idea and very much opposed by everybody, but when it came to a vote, so many of the girls were afraid of offending Candace that they agreed because there was nobody else's father and mother who would let us picnic in their barn, Alice Robinson's barn being full of hay for the winter, and our barn being so dusty the girls all sneeze when they step inside.

They asked me to tell my besetting sin at the very first meeting, and it nearly killed me to do it, because it is such a common greedy one. It is that I can't bear to call the other girls when I have found a thick spot when we are out berrying in the summer time.

After I confessed, which made me dreadfully ashamed, every one of the girls seemed surprised and said that they had never noticed that one but had each thought of something very different that I would be sure to think was my besetting sin. Then Emma Jane said that rather than tell hers she would resign from the Society and miss the picnic. So it made so much trouble that Candace gave up. We struck out that rule from the constitution, and I had told my sin for nothing.

The reason we named ourselves the BOSS is that Minnie Smellie has had her head shaved after scarlet fever and has no braid, so she can't be a member.

I don't want her for a member, but I can't be happy thinking she will feel hurt, and it takes away half the pleasure of belonging to the Society myself and being the president. That, I think, is one main trouble about doing mean and unkind things. You can't do wrong and feel right, or be bad and feel good. If you only could, you could do anything that came into your mind yet always be happy. The other is, that when we hurt others it's not just other people but God, for He made us in His image, even Minnie. This troubles me very much, for I know in my heart that I should always please the Lord.

Minnie Smellie spoils everything she comes into, but I suppose we other girls must either have our hair shaved and call ourselves The Baldheadians or let her be some kind of a special officer in the BOSS. She might be the BITUD member (Braid in the Upper Drawer), for there is where Mrs. Smellie keeps it now that it is cut off.

Winter Thoughts

March 10

It is not such a cold day for March, so I am up in the barn chamber with my coat and hood on and Aunt Jane's waterproof coat and my mittens. Only last week I'd have had to wear my long underwear under my dress, too. After I do three pages, I am going to hide this book away behind the loose board until spring.

Perhaps they get made into icicles on the way, but I do not seem to have many thoughts in the wintertime. The barn chamber is full of thoughts in warm weather. The sky gives them to me, and the trees and flowers and the birds and the river. But now it is always gray and nipping, the branches are bare and the river is frozen. I know this is so, though I can't see the river and fields just now, the door being shut, and the only light being from the window which I can't see out because it's too high, and which doesn't let in much light, because it is covered with cobwebs.

It is too cold to write in my bedroom, there being no stove there. Over the Christmas season, while we kept a fire in the sitting room, I had a few thoughts, but now we use only the airtight stove in the dining room. We sit so close together, Aunt Miranda, Aunt Jane, and I, that I don't dare write in my Thought Book for fear they will ask me to read my secret thoughts to them.

I have just read over the first part of my Thought Book, and I have outgrown it all, just exactly as I have outgrown my last year's drab cashmere sweater.

It is very queer how anybody can change so fast in a few years, but I remember that Emma Jane's cat had kittens the day my book was bought at Watson's Merchantile Store. Mrs. Perkins kept the prettiest white one and asked Abijah Flagg to drown all the rest, which is very sad and morbid. It seems strange to me that cats will go on having kittens when they know what becomes of them! We were very sad about it, but Mrs. Perkins said it was the way of the world and how things had to be, or else the world would soon be full of cats.

Emma Jane's kitten that was born the same day this book was is now quite an old cat who knows the way of the world herself, and how things have to be. So perhaps it is not strange that my Thought Book seems so babyish and foolish to me when I think of all I have gone through and the millions of things I have learned, and how much better I spell than I did only a few years ago when this Thought Book was begun.

My fingers are cold through my mittens, so good-by dear Thought Book, friend of my childhood, now so far behind me! I will hide you where you'll be warm and cosy for the rest of the winter and where nobody can find you in apple blossom time but your affectionate author.

Rebecca Rowena Randall

22

A TRAGEDY IN HATS

E mma Jane Perkins' new winter dress was a blue and green Scotch plaid poplin trimmed with narrow green velvet ribbon and steel nailheads. She had a gray jacket of thick furry cloth with large steel buttons up the front, a pair of green kid gloves, and a gray felt hat with an encircling band of bright green feathers. They began in front with a bird's head and ended behind with a bird's tail, and angels could have desired no more beautiful an outfit. That was her opinion, and it was shared to the full by Rebecca.

But Emma Jane, as Rebecca used to describe years earlier when they both were children, was "a rich blacksmith's daughter," and she, Rebecca, had thought of herself as "a half orphan from a mortgaged farm up Temperance way" since she was still dependent upon her spinster aunts for board, clothes, and schooling. Scotch plaid poplins were obviously not for her, but dark-colored woolen stuffs were, and hand-knit mittens and last winter's coats, bought too large on purpose, were first hemmed, then let down serveral inches by Aunt Miranda to last a second winter.

And how about hats? Was there hope for her there, she wondered, as she walked home from the Perkins house, full of admiration for Emma Jane's winter outfit and loyally trying to keep that admiration free from wicked envy. Her red-winged black hat was her second best, and although it was shabby, she still liked it. But it would *never* do for church, even in Aunt Miranda's strange and never-to-be understood views of suitable clothing.

There was a brown felt turban in existence, if you could call it existence when it had been rained on, snowed on, and hailed on for seasons without number. But the trimmings had at any rate perished quite off the face of the earth — that was one comfort!

Emma Jane had said, rather indiscreetly, that at the Village Hat Shoppe over at Milltown there was a perfectly elegant pink bird breast to be had, a feather breast that began in a perfectly elegant lavender and terminated in a perfectly elegant deep magenta — two colors much in style at that time. If Rebecca were to be required to wear the old brown turban still another winter, would Aunt Miranda hide its shabbiness beneath the lavender-shaded feathers? Would she? That was the question.

Filled with these perplexing thoughts, Rebecca entered the brick house, hung up her knit hood in the entry, and went into the dining room.

Aunt Jane was not there, but Aunt Miranda sat by the window with her lap full of sewing things and a chair piled with cardboard boxes by her side. In one hand was the ancient, battered, brown felt turban, and in the other were the orange and black porcupine quills from Rebecca's last summer's straw hat, from the hat of the summer before that, and the summer before that, and so on back to prehistoric ages of which her childish memory kept no specific record, though she was sure that their neighbors in Riverboro did. Truly this was a sight to chill

the blood of any eager young dreamer who had been looking at brighter plumage!

Miss Sawyer glanced up for a second with a satisfied
expression and then bent her eyes again upon her work. "If
I was going to buy a hat trimming," she said, "I couldn't
select anything better or more economical than these
quills! Your mother had them when she was married, and
you wore them the day you come to the brick house from
the farm. I said to myself then that they looked kind of
outlandish, but I've grown to like 'em now I've got used
to 'em. They've hardly been out o' wear, summer or winter, more'n a month to a time! I declare they do beat all
for service! It don't seem as if your mother could 'a'
chose 'em — Aurelia was always such a poor buyer!

"The black quills are 'bout as good as new, but the
orange ones are gittin' a little mite faded and shabby,"
Aunt Miranda rattled on, pleased with herself. "I wonder if
I couldn't dip all of 'em in shoe blackin'? It seems real
queer to put a porcupine into hat trimmin', though I declare that I don't know jest what the animals are like, it
seems so long since I looked at the pictures of 'em in a
book. I always thought their quills stood out straight and
angry, but these kind o' curls under some at the ends, and
that makes 'em stand the wind better. How do you like
'em on the brown felt?" she asked, inclining her head in a
discriminating attitude and positioning them awkwardly on
the hat with her work-stained hand.

How did she like them on the brown felt indeed?

Miss Sawyer had not been looking at Rebecca, but
Rebecca's eyes were flashing, her bosom heaving, and her
cheeks glowing with sudden rage and despair. All at once
something happened. She forgot that she was speaking to
an older person, forgot that she was dependent, forgot everything but her disappointment at losing the lavender-

feathered breast, remembering nothing but the enchanting, thrilling beauty of Emma Jane Perkins's winter outfit, and suddenly without warning she burst into a torrent of protest.

"I will not wear those hateful porcupine quills again this winter! I will not! It's wicked, *wicked* to expect me to! Oh, how I wish there never had been any porcupines in the world, or that all of them had died before silly, hateful people ever thought of trimming hats with them! They curl round and tickle my ear! They blow against my cheek and sting it like needles! They do look outlandish, you said so yourself a minute ago. Nobody ever had any but only just me! The only porcupine was made into the only quills for me and nobody else! I wish instead of sticking *out* of the nasty beasts, that they stuck *into* them, same as they do into my cheek! I suffer, suffer, *suffer* wearing them and hating them, and they will last forever and forever, and when I'm dead and can't help myself, somebody'll rip them out of my last year's hat and stick them on my head, and I'll be buried in them! Well, when *I* am buried *they* will be, that's one good thing! Oh, if I ever have a child, I'll let her choose her own feathers and not make her wear ugly things like pigs' bristles and porcupine quills!"

When she finished this angry speech, Rebecca vanished like a meteor through the door and down the street, while Miranda Sawyer gasped for breath and prayed to Heaven to help her understand such human whirlwinds as this niece of hers.

This was at three o'clock, and at half-past three Rebecca was kneeling on the rag carpet with her head in her aunt's apron, sobbing her contrition. "Oh, Aunt Miranda, do forgive me if you can. It's the only time I've been bad for months! You know it is! You know you said last week I hadn't been any trouble lately. Something broke inside of me and came tumbling out of my mouth in ugly words!

The porcupine quills make me feel just as a bull does when he sees a red cloth. Nobody understands how I suffer with them!"

Miranda Sawyer had learned a few lessons in the last several years, lessons which were making her a trifle kinder, and at any rate a juster woman that she used to be. When she alighted on the wrong side of her four-poster bed in the morning, or felt an extra touch of rheumatism pain, she was still grim and unyielding. But sometimes a curious sort of melting process seemed to go on within her, when her whole bony structure softened and her eyes grew less angry. At such moments Rebecca used to feel as if a tight iron yoke had been lifted from her shoulders, allowing her to breathe freely and enjoy the sunshine.

"Well," said Aunt Miranda finally, after staring first at Rebecca and then at the porcupine quills as if to find some insight into the situation, "well, I never, since I was born into the world, heerd such a speech as you've spoke, an' I guess there probably won't be another one. You'd better tell the minister what you said and see what he thinks of his prize Sunday school scholar. But I'm too old and tired to scold and fuss and try to train you, same as I did at first. You've apologized, and we won't say no more about it today, but I expect you to show by extry good conduct how sorry you be! You care altogether too much about your looks and your clothes for a child, and you've got a temper that'll certainly land you in state prison one o' these days!"

Rebecca wiped her eyes and laughed aloud. "No, no, Aunt Miranda, it won't, really! That wasn't temper. I don't get angry with *people,* but only once in a long while, with *things*. Like those — cover them up quick before I begin again! I'm all right. Shower's over, sun's out!"

Miss Miranda looked at her searchingly without understanding. Rebecca's state of mind came perilously near to mental illness, she thought. "Have you seen me buying any new bonnets or your Aunt Jane?" she asked cuttingly. "Is there any particular reason why you should dress better than your elders? You might as well know that we're short of cash just now, your Aunt Jane and me, and have no intention of riggin' you out like a Boston society girl."

"Oh-h!" cried Rebecca, the quick tears starting again to her eyes and the color fading out of her cheeks, as she scrambled up from her knees to a seat on the sofa beside her aunt.

"Oh-h! how ashamed I am! Quick, sew those quills on to the brown turban while I'm good! If I can't stand them, I'll make a neat little gingham bag and slip it over them!"

And so the matter ended, not as it customarily did, with cold words on Miss Miranda's part and bitter feelings on Rebecca's, but w̶i̶u̶.̶.̶.̶.̶.̶t gleam of mutual understanding.

Mrs. Cobb, who was a master hand at coloring, dipped the offending quills in brown dye and left them to soak in it all night, not only making them a nice warm color, but somewhat weakening their prickly spines, so that they were not quite as rampantly hideous as before, in Rebecca's opinion. Then Mrs. Perkins went to her bandbox in the attic and gave Miss Dearborn some pale blue velvet with which she bound the brim of the brown turban and made a wonderful rosette, out of which the porcupine's defensive armor sprang, buoyantly and gallantly, like the plume of a medieval king.

Now that Rebecca knew that economy was at the root of some of Aunt Miranda's decisions, she managed to forget the feather hat trim, except in her sleep, where a vision of it had a way of appearing to her, dangling from the ceiling and dazzling her so with its rich color that she used to hope the hatter would sell it so that she might never be tempted with it when she passed the shop window.

ᴣ᷉ ᴣ᷉ ᴣ᷉

One day, not long afterward, Miss Miranda borrowed Mr. Perkins' horse and wagon and took Rebecca with her on a drive to North Riverboro to see about some sausage meat and head cheese. She intended to call on Mrs. Cobb, order a load of pine kindling wood from Mr. Strout on the way, and leave some rags to be braided into a rug with old Mrs. Pease, so that the journey could be made as profitable as possible, consistent with the loss of time and the wear and tear on her second-best silk dress.

The red-winged black hat was, against her will, removed from Rebecca's head just before starting, and the nightmare turban substituted. "You might as well begin to wear it first as last," remarked Miranda, while Jane stood in the side door and sympathized secretly with Rebecca.

"I will!" said Rebecca, ramming the stiff turban down on her head with a vindictive grimace, and snapping the elastic under her long braids, "but it's gonna spoil the whole trip for me." Wisely, Aunt Miranda said no more, except to pass Rebecca the reins as they clambered into the wagon to let her drive the horse, which lightened her spirits considerably.

It was a cold blustering day, with a high wind that promised to bring an early fall of snow. The trees were stripped bare of leaves, the ground was frozen hard, and the wagon wheels rattled noisily over the ruts.

"I'm glad I wore my paisley shawl over my cloak," said Aunt Miranda. "Be you warm enough, Rebecca? Tie that white rabbit fur tighter 'round your neck. The wind fairly blows through my bones. I 'most wish we'd waited till a pleasanter day, for this road is all up hill or down, and we shan't get over the ground fast, it's so rough. Don't forget, when you go into Scott's butcher shop, to say I want all the trimmin's when they send me the pork, for mebbe I can cook out a little mite o' lard. That last load o' pine kindlin's gone turrible quick. I must see if 'Bijah Flagg can't get us some slabs at the sawmill when he hauls for Squire Bean next time. Keep your mind on your drivin', Rebecca, and don't look at the trees and sky so much. It's the same sky and same trees that have been here right along. Go awful slow down this hill and walk the hoss over Cook's Brook bridge, for I always suspicion it's goin' to break down under me, an' I shouldn't want to be dropped into that fast runnin' water this cold day. It'll be froze stiff by this time next week. Hadn't you better get out and lead. . ."

The rest of the sentence was very possibly not vital, but at any rate it was never completed. In the middle of the bridge, a fierce gale of wind whipped Miss Miranda's paisley shawl over her head. The long heavy ends whirled in opposite directions and wrapped themselves tightly about her wavering bonnet. Rebecca held the horsewhip and the reins, and in trying to rescue her struggling aunt, she could not steady her own hat, which was suddenly torn from her head and tossed against the bridge rail, where it trembled and flapped for an instant.

"My hat! Oh, Aunt Miranda, my hateful hat!" cried Rebecca, never remembering at the instant how often she had prayed that the "fretful porcupine" might sometime vanish in this violent manner, since it refused to die a natural death. She had already stopped the horse, so giving her aunt's shawl one last desperate twitch, she slipped out between the wagon wheels and darted in the direction of the hated object, the loss of which had dignified it with a temporary value and importance.

She slipped out between the wagon wheels and darted in the direction of the hated object.

The stiff brown turban rose in the air, then dropped and flew along the bridge. Rebecca pursued as it danced along and stuck between two of the railings. Rebecca flew after it, her long braids floating in the wind.

"Come back! Come back! Don't leave me alone with the team. I won't have it! Come back, and leave your hat!" Miranda had at length extricated herself from the smothering shawl, but she was so blinded by the wind and so confused that she did not measure the financial loss involved in her commands.

Rebecca heard, but her spirit being up in arms, she made one more mad scramble for the vagrant hat which now seemed possessed with an evil spirit, for it flew back and forth and bounded here and there, like a living thing, finally blowing between the horse's front and hind legs, as Rebecca circled, trying to meet it on the other side.

It was no use. As she darted from behind the wheels, the wind gave the hat an extra whirl, and scurrying in the opposite direction, it soared above the bridge rail and disappeared into the rapid white water below.

"Get in again!" cried Miranda, holding on to her bonnet. "You done your best and it can't be helped. I only wish't I'd let you wear your black hat as you wanted to. And I wish't we'd never come on such a day! The shawl has broke the stems of the velvet geraniums in my bonnet, and the wind has blowed away my shawl pin and my back comb. I'd like to give up and turn right back this minute, but I don't like to borrer Perkins' hoss again this month. When we drive through the woods, you can smooth your hair down and tie the rabbit fur over your head and settle what's left of my bonnet. It'll be an expensive errand, this will!"

23

ABIJAH FLAGG'S
GOOD DEED

Not till next morning did Rebecca's heart really begin its song of thanksgiving. Aunt Miranda announced at breakfast, that as Mrs. Perkins was going to Milltown, Rebecca might go too and buy a serviceable hat.

"You mustn't pay over two dollars and a half, and you mustn't get the pink feather breast unless Miz Perkins says, and the hatter says, that it won't fade nor molt. Don't buy a light-colored felt because you'll get sick of it in two or three years, same as you did the brown one. I always liked the shape of the brown one, and you'll never get another trimmin' that'll wear you like them quills."

I hope not! thought Rebecca, as Aunt Miranda instructed her.

"If you had put your elastic under your chin, same as you used to, and not worn it behind because you think it's more grown-up and fashionable, the wind never'd 'a' took the hat off your head, and you wouldn't 'a' lost it. But the mischief's done, and you can go right over to Miz Perkins' now, so you won't miss her nor keep her waitin'. The two dollars and a half is in an envelope side o' the clock."

Rebecca swallowed the last forkful of boiled codfish on her plate, wiped her lips, and rose from her chair happier than the seraphs in Paradise.

The porcupine quills had disappeared from her life and without any fault or violence on her part. She was wholly innocent and virtuous, but nevertheless she was going to have a new hat with the lavender-feathered breast, should the adored object prove, under rigorous examination, to be practically indestructible.

> Whene're I take my walks abroad,
> How many hats I'll see;
> But if they're trimmed with hedgehog quills
> They'll not belong to me!

So she improvised, secretly and ecstatically as she went toward the side entry.

"There's 'Bijah Flagg drivin' in," said Miss Miranda, going to the window. "Step out and see what he's got, Jane. Some passel from the Squire, I guess. It's a paper bag and it may be a punkin, though he wouldn't wrap up a punkin, come to think of it! Shut the dinin' room door, Jane, it's turrible drafty. Make haste, for the Squire's hoss never stan's still a minute 'cept when he's goin'!"

Abijah Flagg alighted and approached the side door with a grin. "Guess what I've got for ye, Becky."

No throb of prophetic soul warned Rebecca of her approaching doom.

"Nodhead apples?" she sparkled, looking as bright and rosy and satin-skinned as an apple herself.

"No. Guess again."

"A flowering geranium?"

"Guess again!"

"Oh! I can't, 'Bijah. I'm just going to Milliken's Mills on an errand, and I'm afraid of missing Mrs. Perkins. Show me quick! Is it really for me, or for Aunt Miranda?"

"Really for you, I guess!" and he opened the large brown paper bag and drew from it the remains of a water-soaked hat! They *were* remains, but there was no doubt of their nature and substance. They had clearly been a hat in the past, and one could even suppose that, when resuscitated, they might again assume their original form in some near and happy future.

Miss Miranda, full of curiosity, joined the group in the side entry at this dramatic moment. "Well, I never!" she exclaimed. "Where, and how on earth did you ever?"

"I was working on the dam at North Riverboro yesterday," chuckled Abijah, with a pleased glance at each of the trio in turn, "an' I seen this little bonnet skippin' over the water jest as Becky does over the road. It's shaped kind o' like a boat, an' gorry, if it wa'n't sailin' jest like a boat! 'Where hev I seen that kind of a brislin' plume?' thinks I."

Where indeed! thought Rebecca stormily.

"Then it come to me that I'd drove that plume to school and drove it to church an' drove it to the fair an' drove it most everywheres on Becky. So I reached out a pole an' ketched it 'fore it got in 'mongst the logs an' come to any damage, an' here it is! The hat's passed in its checks, I guess. Looks kind as if a wet elephant had stepped on it. But the plume's 'bout good as new! I really snatched the hat back for the sake o' the plume."

"It was real good of you, 'Bijah, an' we're all of us obliged to you," said Miranda, as she poised the wet hat on one hand and turned it slowly with the other. "Well, I do say," she exclaimed, "and I guess I've said it before, that of all the wearin' plumes that ever I see, that one's the

wearin'est! Seems though it just wouldn't give up. Look at
the way it's held Miz Cobb's dye. It's about as brown's
when it went into the water."

"Dyed, but not a mite dead," grinned Abijah.

"And I declare," Miranda continued, "when you think
o' the fuss they make about ostriches, killin' 'em off by
hundreds for the sake o' their feathers that'll string out and
spoil in one hard rainstorm, an' all the time lettin' useful
porcupines run round with their quills on. Why I can't
hardly understand it, why hatters haven't found out jest
how good they do last, an' so they won't use 'em for
trimmin'. 'Bijah's right. The hat ain't no more use, Rebecca, but you can buy you another this mornin' — any
color or shape you fancy — an' have Miss Dearborn sew
these brown quills on to it with some kind of a buckle or a
bow, jest to hide the roots. Then you'll be fixed for another season, thanks to 'Bijah."

ه   ه   ه

Uncle Jerry and Aunt Sarah Cobb were made ac-
quainted before very long with the part that Abijah Flagg
had played in Rebecca's affairs, for accompanied by her
teacher, Miss Dearborn, she walked to the old stage
driver's that same afternoon. Taking off her new hat, a
stylish blue felt bonnet, but with the ancient trimming, she
laid it with a flourish upside down on the kitchen table and
left the room, grinning a little more than usual.

Uncle Jerry rose from his seat, and crossing the room,
looked curiously into the hat and found that a circular
paper lining was neatly pinned in the crown, and that it
bore these lines in Rebecca's handwriting, which were
read aloud with great effect by Miss Dearborn, and with
her approval were copied in the Thought Book for the
benefit of posterity:

It was the bristling porcupine,
As he stood on his native heath,
He said, "I'll pluck me
    some immortal quills
And make me up a wreath.
For though I may not live myself
To more than a hundred and ten,
My quills will last till crack of doom,
And maybe after then.
They can be colored blue or green
Or orange, brown, or red,
But often as they may be dyed
They never will be dead."
And so the bristling porcupine
As he stood on his native heath,
Said, "I think I'll pluck me
    some immortal quills
And make me up a wreath."

Uncle Jerry listened with interest and amusement to Rebecca's poem. He listened and chuckled as she told the tale of the horrid porcupine quills and how they had returned when she thought they were forever gone. "Well Becky," he then remarked, "it *is* a han'some new hat, quills or no quills. Sometimes the Lord gives us conditions with His blessin's to teach us humility, I think."

24

RIVERBORO SEWS A FLAG

The flag-raising, a festivity that took place a year before Rebecca entered Wareham Academy and said
good-by to Miss Dearborn and the Riverboro Village
School, was an idea conceived by Mrs. Baxter, wife of the
new minister at Tory Hill Meeting House. There must
have been other flag-raisings in history; even the persons
most interested in this particular one would grudgingly
have allowed that much. But it would have seemed to
them improbable that any such flag-raising as theirs could
twice glorify the same century. Of some pageants it must
be admitted that there can be no duplicates, and the flag-
raising at Riverboro was one of these. So it is small wonder if Rebecca chose it as one of the important dates in her
personal biography.

Mrs. Baxter communicated her patriotic idea of a new
flag to the church's Dorcas Society, proposing that the
women should cut and make it themselves. "It may not be
quite as good as those manufactured in the large cities,"
she said, "but we shall be proud to see our homemade flag
flying in the breeze, and it will mean all the more to the

young voters growing up to remember that their mothers made it with their own hands."

"How would it do to let some of the girls help?" modestly asked Miss Dearborn, the Riverboro teacher. "We might choose the best sewers and let them put in at least a few stitches, so that they can feel they have a share in it."

"Just the thing!" exclaimed Mrs. Baxter. "We can cut the stripes and sew them together, and after we have basted on the white stars, the girls can apply them to the blue ground. We must have it ready for the campaign rally, and we couldn't christen it at a better time than in this presidential election year."

Thus the great enterprise was started, and day by day the preparations went forward in the village.

The boys, as future voters and fighters, demanded an active share in the proceedings and were organized by Squire Bean into a fife-and-drum corps, so that by day and night, martial but inharmonious music woke the echoes, and deafened mothers felt their patriotism oozing out at the soles of their shoes.

Dick Carter was made captain of the corps, for his grandfather had a gold medal given him by Queen Victoria for rescuing 326 passengers from a sinking British vessel. Riverboro thought it high time to pay some graceful tribute to Great Britain in return for her handsome conduct to Captain Nahum Carter, and human imagination could contrive nothing more impressive than a vicarious, posthumous share in the flag-raising.

Ted Perkins tried to be happy in the ranks, though he was offered no official position. "Principally," Mrs. Smellie observed, "because his father's war record wasn't clean. Oh, yes! Bill Perkins went to the war," she continued. "He hid out behind the hencoop when they was draftin', but they found him and took him along. He got into one battle, too,

somehow or 'nother, but he run away from it. He was al-
lers cautious, Bill Perkins was. If he ever seen trouble of
any kind comin' toward him, he was out o' sight 'fore it
got a chance to light. He said eight dollars a month, without bounty, wouldn't pay him to stop Confederate bullets
for. He wouldn't fight a skeeter, Bill wouldn't, but land,
we ain't to war all the time, and he's a good neighbor and
a good blacksmith."

Miss Dearborn was to be the new Statue of Liberty,
recently erected in New York Harbor, and the older girls
of the school were to be the states. Such trade in muslins
and red, white, and blue ribbons had never been known
since "Watson kep' store," and the number of white petticoats hanging out to bleach would have caused the passing
stranger to imagine Riverboro a continual dancing school.

Juvenile goodness, both male and female, reached an
almost impossible height, for parents had only to lift a finger and say, "You shan't go to the flag-raising!" and the
zealous spirit at once pressed itself for new struggles toward the perfect life.

Mr. Jeremiah Cobb had consented to impersonate
Uncle Sam, and he was to drive Liberty and the states to
the raising on the top of his own stage. Meantime the boys
were drilling, the ladies were cutting and basting and
stitching, and the girls were sewing on stars, for the starry
part of the banner was to remain with each of them in turn
until she had performed her share of the work. It was felt
by one and all a fine and splendid service indeed to help in
the making of the flag, and if Rebecca was proud to be of
the chosen ones, so was her Aunt Jane Sawyer, who had
taught her all her delicate stitches.

On a long-looked-for afternoon in August, the minister's
wife drove up to the brick house door and handed out the
great piece of bunting to Rebecca, who received it in her

arms with as much solemnity as if it had been a newborn baby. "I'm so glad!" she sighed happily. "I thought it would never come my turn!"

"You should have had it a week ago, but Huldah Meserve upset an ink bottle over her star, and we had to baste on another one. You are the last, though, and then we shall sew the stars and stripes together. And Seth Strout will get the top of the new flagpole ready for hanging. Just think, it won't be many days before you young people will be pulling the rope with all your strength, the band will be playing, the men will be cheering, and the new flag will go higher and higher, till the red, white, and blue shows against the sky! Look at all the others and make the most beautiful stitches you can. It is your star, you know, and you can even imagine it is your state, and try and have it the best of all. If everybody else is trying to do the same thing with her state, that will make a great country, won't it?"

Rebecca's eyes spoke glad confirmation of the idea. "My star, my state!" she repeated joyously. "Oh, Mrs. Baxter, I'll make such fine stitches you'll think the white grew out of the blue!"

The new minister's wife looked pleased to see her spark kindle a flame in the young heart. "You can sew so much of yourself into your star," she went on in a glad voice that made her so winsome, "that when you are an old lady you can put on your specs and find it among all the others. Good-by! Come up to the parsonage Saturday afternoon. Mr. Baxter wants to see you."

ॐ   ॐ   ॐ

"Judson, help that dear little genius of a Rebecca all you can," Mrs. Baxter told her husband that night, when they were cozily talking in the parsonage parlor. "I don't know what she may or may not come to some day. I only

wish she were ours! If you could have seen her clasp the
flag tight in her arms and put her cheek against it and
watched the tears of feeling start in her eyes when I told
her that her star was her state! I kept whispering to myself,
'Covet not thy neighbor's child!'"

                                                  ᐤ   ᐤ   ᐤ

Daily at four o'clock Rebecca scrubbed her hands almost to the bone, brushed her hair, and otherwise prepared
herself in body, mind, and spirit for the consecrated labor
of sewing on her star. All the time that her needle cautiously, conscientiously formed the tiny stitches she was
making rhymes in her head, her favorite achievement
being this:

> Your star, my star, all our stars together,
> They make the dear old banner proud
> To float in the bright fall weather.

There was much discussion as to which of the girls
should impersonate the state of Maine at the flag-raising,
for that was felt to be the highest honor by the members of
the committee.

Alice Robinson was the prettiest child in the village,
but she was very shy and by no means a general favorite.

Minnie Smellie possessed the handsomest dress and a
pair of white slippers and open work stockings that nearly
carried the day. Still, she was accounted so immature that
if she should suck her thumb in the very middle of the
exercises nobody'd be surprised.

Huldah Meserve was next voted upon, and the fact that
if she were not chosen her father might withdraw his subscription to the brass band fund was a matter for grave
consideration. "But I kind o' hate to have such a giggler
for the state of Maine," remarked Mrs. Burbank.

"How would Rebecca Randall do for Maine, and let her speak some of her verses?" suggested the new minister's wife, who could she have had her way, would have given all the prominent parts to Rebecca, from Uncle Sam down.

So, beauty, fashion, and wealth having been tried and found wanting, the committee discussed the claims of talent, and it transpired that to Rebecca fell the chief plum in the pudding. It was a tribute to her gifts that there was no jealousy or envy among the other girls, for they readily conceded her special fitness for the role.

Her life had not been pressed down full to the brim of pleasures, and Rebecca had a sort of distrust of joy in the bud. Not until she saw joy in full radiance of bloom did she dare embrace it. She would have agreed heartily with the poet who said:

> Not by appointment do we meet delight
> And joy; they heed not our expectancy;
> But round some corner in the streets of life
> They on a sudden clasp us with a smile.

For many nights before the raising when she went to her bed she said to herself, after she had finished her prayers, "It can't be true that I'm chosen for the state of Maine! It just *can't* be true! Nobody could be good *enough*, but oh, I'll try to be as good as I can! To be going to be the State of Maine! Oh! I must pray *hard* to God to keep me meek and humble!"

25

THE SIMPSONS DEPART

The flag was to be raised on a Tuesday, and on the previous Sunday the children of Riverboro learned that Clara Belle Simpson was coming back from Acreville, where her family had moved earlier in the summer. She would live with Mrs. Fogg and take care of the Fogg baby, called by the neighborhood boys "the Fogg Horn," on account of his shrill bawling.

Clara Belle, if she were left wholly out of the festivities, would be the only girl of suitable age to be thus slighted. It seemed clear that she would never recover from such a blow. But under all the circumstances, would she be allowed to join in the procession? Even Rebecca the optimist feared she would not, and the committee confirmed her fears by saying that the daughter of that thievin' Abner Simpson certainly could not take any prominent part in the ceremony, but they surely hoped that Mrs. Fogg would allow her to watch it.

The departure of the Simpsons, bag and baggage, including the banquet lamp, their most conspicuous possession, had truly been a milestone in the cycle of life in Riverboro. Rebecca found it delightful at first to be rid of Seesaw's embarrassing presence, for he had continually

213

sought her unwilling affections, but otherwise the loss of several playmates at one fell swoop made rather a gap in Riverboro's younger set.

The Simpsons' move had been precipitated by the town's foreclosure on their meager estate for nonpayment of taxes and the sale of their tumbledown house and its three acres for less than was owed. The selectmen decided that seven years, like the itch, was long enough to tolerate a tribe of paupers more properly belonging to another community in another county.

Mr. Simpson had come home from the York County Jail just in time to move his wife and children back to the town that had given them birth, a town by no means waiting with open arms to receive them. The Simpsons' moving was presided over by the village constable and somewhat anxiously watched by the entire neighborhood, but in spite of all precautions, a pulpit chair, several kerosene lamps, and a small stove disappeared from the church and were successfully swapped in the course of Mr. Simpson's driving his family from the old home to their new.

It gave Rebecca and Emma Jane hours of sorrow to learn later that a certain village along the way of Abner Simpson's journey had acquired, through the dealing of an ambitious young minister, a magnificent lamp for its new church parlor. No money changed hands in the operation, for the minister succeeded in getting the lamp for an old bicycle.

After Abner Simpson, urged by the town authorities, took his wife and seven children away from Riverboro to Acreville, just over the border in the next county, Riverboro citizens once again went to bed leaving their barn and shed doors unfastened, and drew long breaths of gratitude to the Lord.

Squire Bean had been Simpson's nearest neighbor, and he had once conceived the novel idea of paying Simpson five dollars a year not to steal from him. The bargain was struck and adhered to religiously for a year, but on the second of January, Mr. Simpson announced the verbal contract as formally broken. "I didn't know what I was doin' when I made a deal with you, Squire," he urged. "In the first place, it's a slur to my reputation and an injury to my self-respect. Secondly, it's a nervous strain on me; and thirdly, five dollars don't pay me!"

Squire Bean was so struck with the unique and convincing nature of these arguments that he could scarcely restrain his admiration, and he confessed to himself afterward that unless Simpson's mental attitude could be changed, he was perhaps a fitter subject for psychology than for prison.

Abner was a most unusual thief, and he conducted his operations with a tact and neighborly consideration none too common in the profession. He would never steal a man's scythe in haying time, nor his buffalo-hide lap robe in the coldest of the winter. The picking of a lock offered no attractions to him. "I ain't no burglar," he would have scornfully asserted. Bill Perkins once wryly observed that though "Simpson ain't no lawyer" he knew that "breakin' and enterin' is five years in state prison, first offense."

A strange horse and wagon hitched by the roadside was the most flagrant of Simpson's thefts. But it was the small things — the hatchet or ax on the chopping block, the tin pans sunning at the side door, a stray garment bleaching on the grass, a hoe, rake, shovel, or a bag of early potatoes — these tempted him most sorely. And these appealed to him not so much for their intrinsic value as because they were so excellently adapted to swapping. The swapping was really the enjoyable part of the procedure;

the theft was only a sad but necessary preliminary. For if Abner himself had been a man of sufficient property to carry on his business operations independently, it is doubtful if he would have helped himself so freely to his neighbors' goods.

Riverboro regretted the loss of Mrs. Simpson, who was useful in scrubbing, cleaning, and washing, and she was thought to exercise some influence over her predatory spouse. There was a story of their early married life, when they had a farm—a story to the effect that Mrs. Simpson always rode on every load of hay that her husband took to market in Milltown with the view of keeping him sober through the day. It was said that after he turned out of the country road and approached the village, he used to bury the docile lady in the load. He would then drive onto the scales, have the weight of the hay entered in the buyer's book, take his horse to the stable for feed and water, and when opportunity offered, he would assist the hot and panting Mrs. Simpson out of the back of the rack and gallantly brush the chaff from her person. For this reason it was always asserted that Abner Simpson sold his wife every time he went to Milltown, but the story was never fully substantiated. And it was the only suspected blot on meek Mrs. Simpson's personal reputation.

As for the Simpson children, they were missed chiefly as familiar figures by the roadside. But Rebecca honestly loved Clara Belle in spite of her Aunt Miranda's opposition to the friendship. Rebecca's "taste for low company" was a source of continual anxiety to her aunt.

"Anything that's human flesh is good enough for her!" Miranda groaned to Jane. "She'll ride with the rag, sack, and bottle peddler just as quick as she would with the minister. She always sets beside the most wiggly young-uns at Sunday school. And she's forever riggin' and unriggin' that dirty Simpson baby! She reminds me of a puppy that'll always go to everybody that'll have him!"

&a &a &a

It was thought very kindly of Mrs. Fogg that she sent for Clara Belle to live with her and go to school part of the year. "She'll be useful," said Mrs. Fogg. "And she'll be out of her father's way and so keep honest, though she's so awful homely, I've no fears for her. A girl with her red hair, freckles, and cross-eyes can't fall into no kind of sin, I don't believe."

Mrs. Fogg requested that Clara Belle should take her journey from Acreville by stagecoach, so she was disturbed to receive word on Sunday that Mr. Simpson had borrowed a good horse and buggy from a new acquaintance and would himself drive the girl from Acreville to Riverboro, a distance of thirteen miles. That he would arrive in their vicinity on the very night before the flag-raising was thought by Riverboro to be a public misfortune. Several residents hastily determined to deny themselves a sight of the festivities so as to remain home watching their property.

26

REBECCA SAVES THE COLORS

O n Monday afternoon the children were rehearsing their songs at the church. As Rebecca came out on the broad wooden steps, she watched Mrs. Peter Meserve's buggy until it went out of sight, for in front, wrapped in a cotton sheet, lay the precious flag. After a few chattering goodbyes and weather prophecies with the other girls, she started on her homeward walk, dropping in at the parsonage to read her poetry to the minister.

He welcomed her gladly as she removed her white cotton gloves, which she had hastily slipped on outside the door for ceremony, and pushed back the funny hat with the porcupine quills.

"You've heard the beginning, Mr. Baxter, now will you please tell me if you like the last verse?" she asked, taking out her paper. "I've only read it to Alice Robinson, and I think perhaps she can never be a poet, though she's a splendid writer. Last year when she was thirteen, she wrote a birthday poem to herself, and she made *natal* rhyme with *Milton,* which, of course, it wouldn't. I remember every verse ended:

This is my day so natal
And I will follow Milton.

The minister could scarcely refrain from smiling, but he controlled himself that he might lose none of Rebecca's observation. When she was perfectly at ease, unwatched and uncriticized, she was a marvelous companion.

"The name of the poem is going to be 'My Star,'" she continued, "and Mrs. Baxter gave me all the ideas. But somehow there's a kind of magicness when they get into poetry. Don't you think so?"

"It has often been so remarked in different words," agreed the minister.

"Mrs. Baxter said that each star was a state, and if each state did its best, we should have a splendid country. Then once she said that we ought to be glad the Civil War is over, and the states are all at peace together. And I thought Miss Liberty must be glad, too, for Miss Dearborn says she's like a mother to all the states. So I'm going to have it end like this—I didn't write it, it just came into my head while I was working on my star."

> For it's your star, my star, all the stars
>   together,
> That make our country's flag so proud
> To float in the bright fall weather.
> Northern stars, Southern stars, stars of the
>   East and West,
> Side by side they lie at peace
> On the dear flag's mother breast.

'*Oh, many are the poets that are sown by Nature,*' thought the minister, quoting Wordsworth to himself. *And I wonder what becomes of them?* "That's a pretty idea, Rebecca, and I don't know whether you or my wife ought to have the more praise," said Reverend Baxter as Rebecca rose to go.

           *   *   *

Rebecca walked rapidly along in the gathering twilight, thinking of the events of tomorrow. As she approached the turning on the left called the Old Acreville Road, she saw a white horse and wagon driven by a man with rakish, flapping, Panama hat, come rapidly around the turn and disappear over the long hills leading down to the falls, where the road crossed the bridge and turned through Riverboro Village. There was no mistaking him. There never was another Abner Simpson, with his lean height, his bushy reddish hair, the gay cock of his hat, and the long, pirate-like, upturned mustaches, which the boys used to say were used as hat racks by the Simpson children at night. The Old Acreville Road ran past Mrs. Fogg's house, so he must have left Clara Belle there. Rebecca's heart glowed to think that her poor little friend need not miss the flag-raising.

She began to run now, fearful of being late for supper, and she covered the ground to the falls in a brief time. As she crossed the bridge, she again saw Abner Simpson's team drawn up at the village watering trough. As she came a little nearer and mustered courage to ask Abner how his family was doing, her quick eye caught sight of something unexpected. A gust of wind blew up a corner of a linen lap robe in the back of the wagon, and underneath it she distinctly saw the white-sheeted bundle that held the flag — the bundle with a tiny, tiny spot of red bunting peeping out at one corner. It is true she had eaten, slept, dreamed red, white, and blue for weeks, but there was no mistaking the evidence of her senses. The idolized flag, longed for, worked for, sewed for flag — that flag was in the back of

Abner Simpson's wagon. And if so, what would become of the raising?

Acting on blind impulse, she ran toward the watering trough, calling out in her clear treble, "Mr. Simpson! Oh, Mr. Simpson, will you let me ride a piece with you and hear all about Clara Belle? I'm going part way over to Milltown on an errand!"

Mr. Simpson turned round in his seat and cried heartily, "Certain sure I will!" for Rebecca had always been a favorite with him. "Climb right in! How's everybody? Glad to see ye! The folks talk about ye from sunup to sundown, and Clara Belle can't wait for a sight of ye!"

Rebecca scrambled up, trembling and pale with excitement. She did not in the least know what was going to happen, but she was sure that the flag, when in the enemy's country, must at least be a little safer with the state of Maine sitting on top of it!

Mr. Simpson rattled on about Acreville, the house he lived in, the pond in front of it, Mrs. Simpson's health, and various items of news about the children, and his personal misfortunes. He asked no replies, so this gave the inexperienced soldier a few seconds to plan her campaign. There were three houses to pass — the Browns' at the corner, the Millikens', and the Robinsons' on the brow of the hill. If Mr. Robinson were in the front yard, she might tell Mr. Simpson to hold the horse's head while she got out of the wagon. Then she might fly to the back before Mr. Simpson could realize the situation, and dragging out the precious bundle, sit on it hard, while Hillard Robinson settled the matter of ownership with Mr. Simpson.

This was feasible, but it meant a quarrel between the two men, who held an ancient grudge against each other. And Mr. Simpson was a valiant fighter, as the various sheriffs who had attempted to arrest him could certainly testify. It also meant that everybody in the village would hear of the incident, and poor Clara Belle would again be branded as the child of a thief.

Another idea danced into her excited brain — such a clever one she could hardly believe it hers. She might call Mr. Robinson to the wagon and when he came close to the wheels she might say, all of a sudden, "Please take the flag out of the back of the wagon, Mr. Robinson. We have brought it here for you to keep overnight." Mr. Simpson might be so surprised that he would give up his prize rather than be suspected of stealing.

But as they neared the Robinsons' house, there was not a sign of life to be seen.

The road now passed through thick pine woods with no dwelling in sight. It was growing dusk, and Rebecca was riding along the lonely way with a person who was generally called Slippery Simpson. Not a thought of fear crossed her mind except fear of losing the flag. She knew Mr. Simpson well, and a pleasanter man was seldom to be met. She recalled an afternoon when he came home and surprised the whole school playing the Revolutionary War in his helter-skelter dooryard. The way in which he had joined the British forces and impersonated General Burgoyne had greatly endeared him to her. The only difficulty was to find proper words for her delicate mission, for if Mr. Simpson's anger were aroused, he would push her out of the wagon and drive away with the flag.

Perhaps if she led the conversation in the right direction, an opportunity would present itself. Rebecca well remembered how Emma Jane Perkins had failed to convert Jacob Moody, simply because she failed to properly lead up to the delicate question of his manner of life. Clearing her throat nervously, she began, "Is it likely to be fair tomorrow?"

*It was growing dusk, and Rebecca was riding
along the lonely way with a person who was
generally called Slippery Simpson.*

"Guess so; clear as a bell. What's on foot? A picnic?"

"No. We're to have a grand flag-raising!"

"That so? Where?"

"The village and the folks from all the country 'round are to meet together and have a rally and raise the flag on the green in front of Tory Hill Church. There'll be a brass band and speakers, and the mayor of Portland will be there, and the man that will be governor if he's elected, and a dinner in the Grange Hall, and we girls are chosen to raise the flag.

"I hope Mrs. Fogg will take Clara Belle," Rebecca continued, "for it will be splendid to look at! Mr. Cobb is going to be Uncle Sam and drive us on the stage. Miss Dearborn—Clara Belle's old teacher, you know—is going to be the Statue of Liberty, and the girls will be the states of the Union, and oh, Mr. Simpson, I am the one to be the state of Maine!"

Mr. Simpson flourished his horsewhip and gave a loud, hearty laugh. Then he turned in his seat and regarded Rebecca curiously. "You're kind o' small, hain't ye, for so big a state as this one?" he asked.

"Any of us would be too small," replied Rebecca with dignity, "but the committee asked me, and I am going to try hard to do well. And I'm nearly fifteen!"

The tragic thought that there might be no occasion for anybody to do anything, well or ill, suddenly overcame her here, and putting her hand on Mr. Simpson's sleeve, she attacked the subject directly and courageously.

"Oh, Mr. Simpson, dear Mr. Simpson, it's such a mortifying subject I can't bear to say anything about it, but please give us back our flag! Don't, *don't* take it over to Acreville, Mr. Simpson! We've worked so long to make it, and it was so hard getting the money for the bunting! Wait a minute, please. Don't be angry, and don't say no just

yet, till I explain more. It'll be so dreadful for everybody
to get there tomorrow morning and find no flag to raise,
and the band and the mayor all disappointed, and the little
children crying, with their new muslin dresses all bought
for nothing! Oh dear Mr. Simpson, please don't take our
flag away from us!"

The astonished Abner pulled his mustaches. "But I
don't know what you're drivin' at!" he exclaimed. "Who's
got yer flag? *I* hain't."

Could duplicity, deceit, and infamy go any further, Rebecca wondered. And her soul filling with righteous wrath,
she cast discretion to the winds and spoke a little more
plainly, bending her great swimming eyes on the now embarrassed Abner, who looked like an angleworm wriggling
on a hook.

"Mr. Simpson, how can you say that, when I saw the
flag in the back of your wagon myself when you stopped
to water the horse? It's wicked of you to take it, and I
cannot bear it! If you keep it, you'll have to keep me, for I
won't be parted from it! I can't fight like the boys, but I
can pinch and scratch, and I *will* scratch, just like a pan-
ther. I'll lie right down on my star and not move if I starve
to death!"

"Look here, hold your hosses 'n' don't cry till you git
something to cry about!" shouted the outraged Abner, to
whom a clue had just come. Leaning over the wagon seat
he caught hold of a corner of the white sheet and dragged
up the bundle, scooping off Rebecca's hat in the process
and almost burying her in bunting.

She caught the treasure passionately to her heart and
stifled her sobs in it, while Abner exclaimed, "I swan to
man, if that hain't a flag! Well, in that case you're good
and welcome to it! Land! I seen that bundle lyin' in the
middle o' the road and I says to myself, that's somebody's

washin' and I'd better pick it up and leave it at the post office to be claimed, 'n' all the time it was a flag!"

This was the Simpsonian version of the matter, the fact being that a white-covered bundle lying on the Meserves' front steps had attracted his practiced eye. Slipping in at the open gate, he had swiftly and deftly removed it to his wagon, thinking if it were clean clothes it would be extremely useful in his next trading venture.

Rebecca was a practical girl, and it seemed to her almost impossible that so heavy a bundle should fall out of Mrs. Meserve's buggy and not be noticed. But she hoped that Mr. Simpson was telling the truth, and she was too glad and grateful to doubt anyone at the moment.

"Thank you, thank you ever so much, Mr. Simpson. You're the nicest, kindest, politest man I ever knew, and all the girls will be so pleased you gave us back the flag, and so will the Dorcas Society. They'll be sure to write you a letter of thanks."

"Tell 'em not to bother 'bout any thanks," said Simpson, beaming virtuously. "But land! I'm glad 'twas me that happened to see that bundle in the road and take the trouble to pick it up."

"Can I get out now, please?" asked Rebecca. "I want to go back, for Mrs. Meserve will be dreadfully nervous when she finds out she dropped the flag, and she has heart trouble."

"No, you don't," objected Mr. Simpson gallantly, turning the horse. "Do you think I'd let a little creeter like you lug that great heavy bundle? I hain't got time to go back to Meserves', but I'll take you to the corner and dump you there, flag 'n' all, and you can get some o' the menfolks to carry it the rest of the way. You'll wear it out, huggin' it so!"

"I helped make it and I adore it!" said Rebecca, who was in a high-pitched and grandiloquent mood. "Why, don't *you* like it? It's your country's flag."

Simpson smiled an indulgent smile and looked a trifle bored at these frequent appeals to his extremely rusty higher feelings. "I don' know's I've got any partic'lar int'rest in the country," he remarked languidly. "I know I don't owe nothin' to it, nor own nothin' in it!"

"You own a star on the flag, same as everybody," argued Rebecca, "and you own a state, too, like all of us!"

"Land! I wish't I did! Or even a quarter-section farm!" sighed Mr. Simpson, feeling somehow a little more poverty-stricken and discouraged than usual.

As they approached the corner where four crossroads met, the whole neighborhood seemed to be on hand. Mr. Simpson suddenly regretted his chivalrous escort of Rebecca, especially when an excited lady wringing her hands turned out to be Mrs. Peter Meserve accompanied by Huldah, the Browns, Mrs. Milliken, Abijah Flagg, and Miss Dearborn.

"Do you know anything about the new flag, Rebecca?" shrieked Mrs. Meserve, too agitated at the moment to notice with whom she was riding.

"It's right here in my lap, all safe," responded Rebecca joyously.

"You careless, meddlesome young one, to take it off my steps where I left it just long enough to go round to the back and hunt up my door key! You've given me a fit of sickness with my weak heart, and what business was it of yours? I believe you think you *own* the flag! Hand it over to me this minute!"

Rebecca was climbing down during this torrent of language, but as she turned she flashed one look of knowledge at the false Simpson, a look that went through him from head to foot, as if it were carried by electricity. Fury mounted to his brain, and as soon as she was safely out from between the wheels, he stood up in the wagon and flung the flag out in the road in the midst of the excited group.

"Take it, you pious, parsimonious, flag-raisin' crew!" he roared. "Rebecca never took the flag. I found it in the road, I say!"

"You never no such a thing!" exclaimed Mrs. Meserve. "You found it on the doorsteps by my flower garden!"

"Mebbe 't was your garden, but it was so chock full o' weeds I thought 't was the road," retorted Abner. "I vow I wouldn't 'a' given the old rag back to one o' you, not if you begged me on your bended knees! But Rebecca's a friend o' my folks and can do with flag's she's a-mind to, and the rest o' ye can go to thunder." Simpson made a sharp turn, gave the gaunt white horse a lash with the whip, and disappeared in a cloud of dust before the astonished Mr. Brown, the only man in the party, had a thought of collaring him.

"I'm sorry I spoke so quick, Rebecca," said Mrs. Meserve, greatly mortified at the situation. "But don't you believe a word that lyin' critter said! He did steal it off my doorstep, and how did you come to be ridin' and consortin' with him? I believe it would kill your Aunt Miranda if she should hear about it!"

Miss Dearborn put a sheltering arm around Rebecca as Mr. Brown picked up the flag and dusted and folded it. "I'm willing she should hear about it," Rebecca answered. "I didn't do anything to be ashamed of. I saw the flag in the back of Mr. Simpson's wagon, and I just followed it. There weren't any men or Dorcases to take care of it, and so it fell to me! You wouldn't have had me let it out of my sight, would you, and we going to raise it tomorrow morning?"

"Rebecca's perfectly right, Mrs. Meserve!" said her teacher proudly. "And it's lucky there was somebody quick witted enough to ride and consort with Mr. Simpson! I don't know what the village will think, but seems to me the town clerk might write down in his book, *'This day the state of Maine saved the flag!'*"

27

THE STATE
O' MAINE GIRL

M aine—Rebecca—did shine as a star in our country's
flag should, but not without a tarnish which almost
caused her to fall from the firmament of the states. Alice
Robinson spent the night before the flag-raising with Rebecca. And when the bedroom door closed upon the two
girls, Alice announced her intention of doing up Rebecca's
front hair in leads and rags, and braiding the back in six
tight, wetted braids.

"Aunt Miranda says you might as well set the nap on
the parlor rug as set my hair," said Rebecca cautiously.
But Alice was persistent. "You'll look like an Injun if I
don't!"

"I am the state of Maine. It *all* belonged to the Indians
once!" Rebecca remarked defensively, for she was curiously shy about discussing her personal appearance.

"And your wreath of little pine cones won't set decent
without crimps," Alice argued.

Rebecca glanced in the cracked looking glass and met
what she considered an accusing lack of beauty, a sight
that always either saddened or enraged her according to

circumstances. Then she sat down resignedly and began to help Alice in the work of making the state of Maine fit to be seen at the flag-raising.

Neither of the girls was an expert hairdresser, and at the end of the hour, when the sixth braid was tied and Rebecca had given one last shuddering look in the mirror, both were ready to weep with fatigue.

Rebecca blew the lamp out, and Alice soon went to sleep, but Rebecca herself tossed on her pillow, its goose-feathered softness all dented by the heavy, cruel lead knobs and the hard knots of twisted rags. She slipped out of bed and walked to and fro, holding her aching head with both hands. Finally she leaned on the windowsill, watching the weather vane swimming in the moonlight as it cast its shadow across Alice's barn on the distant hill. She breathed in the fragrance of the ripening apples in the orchard beneath her window until her restlessness subsided under the clear, starry beauty of the night.

At six in the morning the girls were out of bed, for Alice could hardly wait until Rebecca's hair was taken down, she was so eager to see the result of her labors. The leads and rags were painfully removed, together with much hair, and the operation was punctuated by a series of squeaks, squeals, and shrieks on the part of Rebecca and a series of warnings from Alice, who wished the preliminaries to be kept secret from the aunts, that they might more fully appreciate the radiant result. Then came the unbraiding, and then, dramatic moment, the combing out, a difficult, not to say impossible process, in which the hairs that had resisted the earlier tortures almost gave up the ghost.

The long front strands had been wound up from various angles and by various methods, so that when released they assumed the strangest, most obstinate, most unexpected attitudes. When the comb was dragged through the last braid, the wild, tortured, electric hairs followed, then rebounded from it in a bristling, snarling tangle. Massachusetts — Alice — gave one encompassing glance at the state o' Maine's head and announced her intention of going home to breakfast! She suddenly and without explanation felt that meeting Miss Miranda Sawyer at the morning meal would not mend matters in the least. So slipping out the side door, she ran up Guide Board Hill as fast as her legs would carry her.

The state o' Maine, deserted and somewhat unnerved, sat down before the glass and attacked her hair doggedly and with set lips, working over it with her brush until Miss Jane called her to breakfast. With a boldness born of despair, she entered the dining room where her aunts were already seated at the table. To draw fire, Rebecca whistled a few bars of a dance tune she had once heard Seesaw Simpson play on his harmonica, but this only attracted more attention instead of diverting it. There was a moment of silence as the grotesque figure of Maine was fully taken in by the aunts. Then came a moan from Jane and a groan from Miranda.

"What have you done to yourself?" asked Miranda sternly.

"Made an effort to be beautiful and failed!" jauntily replied Rebecca, but she was too miserable to keep up the fiction. "Oh, Aunt Miranda, don't scold. I'm so unhappy! Alice and I rolled up my hair to curl it for the flag-raising. She said it was so straight I looked like an Indian!"

"Mebbe you did," vigorously agreed Miranda, "but at any rate you looked like a Christian Injun, 'n' now you look like a heathen Injun. That's all the difference I can see. Did you want a flag raisin' or a hair-raisin'? What can we do with her, Jane; between now and nine o'clock?"

"We'll all go out to the pump just as soon as we're through breakfast," answered Jane soothingly. "We can accomplish consid'rable with water an' force."

Rebecca nibbled her corn cake, her tearful eyes cast on her plate and her chin quivering. "Don't you cry and red your eyes up," chided Miranda quite kindly. "The minute you've eaten enough, run up and get your stiffest hairbrush and coarsest comb and meet us at the back door."

"I wouldn't care how bad I looked," said Rebecca, "but I can't bear to be so frightful that I shame the state of Maine!"

Oh, what an hour followed this cry! To be dipped in the rain barrel, soused again and again. To be held under the spout by one aunt and pumped on by the other, the water ice-cold from the depths of the well, to be rubbed furiously with rough roller towels, to be dried with hot flannels! At the close of an hour, the ends of the long hair still stood straight out, the braids having been turned up two inches by Alice and tied hard in that position with linen thread.

"Get out the ironing board, Jane," cried Miranda, to whom opposition served as a tonic, "and move that flatiron onto the front o' the stove. Rebecca, set yourself down in that low chair beside the board, and Jane, you spread out her hair on it and cover it up with brown paper. Don't cringe, Rebecca. The worst's over, and you've borne up real good! I'll be careful not to pull your hair nor scorch you, and oh, *how* I'd like to have Alice Robinson acrost my knee and a good strip o' cedar shingle in my right hand!

"There, you're all ironed out, and your Aunt Jane can help you put on your white dress and braid your hair up again good and tight. Perhaps you won't be the homeliest of the states, after all. But when I seen you comin' in to breakfast, I said to myself, 'I guess if Maine ever looked like that, it wouldn't never 'a' been admitted into the Union!'"

When Uncle Sam and the stagecoach drew up to the brick house with a grand swing and a flourish of his whip, most of the states were already in their places on the luggage rack on top. Words fail to describe the gallant bearing of the horses, their bridles gaily trimmed and their harnesses dotted with little flags. The stage windows were hung in bunting, and from within beamed the Statue of Liberty, looking out from the bright frame as if proud of her freight of loyal children and teens. Patriotic streamers floated from the whip, from the dashboard, and from the coach's rumble seat, and the effect was something to stimulate the least patriotic citizen.

Rebecca came out on the steps, and Aunt Jane brought a chair to assist in the ascent to the roof of the coach. Miss Dearborn peeped from the stagecoach window and gave a despairing look at her favorite. What had happened to her? Had her head been put through a wringer? Why were her eyes red and swollen? Miss Dearborn determined right then to take her behind the trees in the pine grove and give her some finishing touches that her skillful fingers fairly itched to bestow.

The stage started, and as the roadside pageant grew livelier and livelier, Rebecca began to brighten and look prettier, for most of her beautifying came from within. The people, walking, driving, or standing on their doorsteps, cheered Uncle Sam's coach with its freight of gossamer-muslined, fluttering-ribboned girls, and just behind came a gorgeously decorated, high-wheeled hayrack driven by Abijah Flagg bearing the jolly but inharmonious fife-and-drum corps.

Was there ever such a golden day! Such crystal air! Such mellow sunshine! Such a merry Uncle Sam! The stage drew up at a spot near a pine grove by the church, and while the crowd was gathering, the children waited for the moment to arrive when they should march to the platform.

As soon as Miss Dearborn could get her alone, she whispered to Rebecca, "Come behind the trees with me! I want to make you prettier!" Rebecca thought she had suffered enough from that process already during the last twelve hours, but she followed her teacher.

Miss Dearborn's principle virtues were devotion to children and ability to gain their love, and a power of evolving a schoolroom order so natural, cheery, serene, and peaceful that it gave the beholder a certain sense of being in a school-district heaven. She was poor in arithmetic and weak in geometry, but if you gave her a rose, a bit of ribbon, and a seven-by-nine looking glass, she could make herself as pretty as a pink in two minutes.

Safely sheltered behind the pines, Miss Dearborn began to practice her mysterious feminine arts. She flew at Rebecca's tight braids, opened the strands and rebraided them loosely. She bit and tore the red, white, and blue ribbon in two and tied the braids separately. Then with nimble fingers she pulled out the little tendrils of hair behind Rebecca's ears and around the nape of her neck. After a glance of acute disapproval directed at the stiff balloon skirt, she knelt on the ground and gave a strenuous embrace to Rebecca's knees, murmuring between her hugs, "Starch must be cheap at the brick house!"

There followed great pinchings of ruffles. Miss Dearborn's fingers, that could never hold a hickory switch nor snap children's ears, proved to be incomparable as fluting irons.

Next, the sash was scornfully untied and tightened to suggest something resembling a waist. The bows that had been squat, dowdy, and spiritless, were given tweaks, flirts, bracing little pokes and dabs, till, acknowledging a master hand, they stood up—piquant, pert, smart, alert.

Pride of bearing was now infused into the flattened lace at the neck, and a pin, removed at some sacrifice from her own outfit, was darned in at the back to prevent any cowardly lapsing.

The short white cotton gloves that called attention to Rebecca's deeply tanned wrists and arms were stripped off and put in her own pocket. Then the wreath of pine cones was adjusted at a rakish angle, and the hair was pulled softly into a fluffy frame. Finally, as she met Rebecca's grateful eyes, she gave her two approving, triumphant kisses on the cheeks. In a second her sensitive face lighted into happiness. Pleased dimples appeared on her cheeks, her mouth became as red as a rose, and the little fright that had walked behind the pine tree stepped out on the other side as Rebecca the Lovely.

Now all was ready. The fife-and-drum corps led the way, and the states followed, but what actually happened Rebecca never knew. She lived through the hours in a waking dream. Every little detail was a facet of light that reflected sparkles, and among them all she was fairly dazzled. The brass band played inspiring strains, the mayor of Portland spoke eloquently on great themes, the people cheered, then the rope on which so much depended was put into the children's hands. Then they applied superhuman strength to their task, and the grand flag mounted, mounted smoothly and steadily. It slowly unwound and stretched itself into the brisk New England breeze with a smart snap until its splendid size and beauty were revealed against the maples and pines and blue skies.

Then, after cheers upon cheers and after the church choir offered a patriotic rendering of "America"—by Maine's own hymn writer, Samuel Francis Smith—the state of Maine mounted her platform, vaguely conscious that she was to recite a poem, though for the life of her she could not remember a single word.

"Speak up loud and clear, Becky," whispered Uncle Sam from the front row, but she could scarcely hear her own voice when, tremblingly, she began the first line. After that she gathered strength, and the poem seemed to say itself while the dream went on.

Rebecca saw Adam Ladd leaning against a tree. Aunt Jane and Aunt Miranda palpitated with nervousness, and Clara Belle Simpson gazed at her in adoration from a seat on the side.

And in the far, far distance, on the very outskirts of the crowd, a man stood in a wagon—a tall, loose-jointed man with red upturned mustaches, and a gaunt white horse turned toward the Acreville Road. Abner Simpson lifted his vagrant, shifting gaze to the flag's softly fluttering folds and its splendid massing of colors, thinking, *I don't know's anybody'd ought to steal a flag. The thunderin' idjuts seem to set such store by it, and what is it, anyway? Nothing but a sheet o' buntin'!*

Nothing but a sheet of bunting? He looked curiously at the rapt faces of the mothers, their babies asleep in their arms. At the parted lips and shining eyes of the children, at Cap'n Lord, who had nearly starved to death in Libby prison during the Civil War, and at Nat Strout, who had lost an arm in the Battle of Bull Run while defending his nation's capitol. He gazed at the friendly, jostling crowd of farmers—happy, eager, absorbed, their throats ready to burst with cheers. Then the breeze swerved, and he heard Rebecca's clear voice saying:

For it's your star, my star, all the stars
   together,
That make our country's flag so proud
To float in the bright fall weather!

Talk about stars! She's got a couple of 'em right in her
head, thought Simpson. *Spunky little creature, too, settin'*
up in my wagon lookin' bout's big as a pint o' cider, but
keepin' right after the goods! I vow I'm 'bout sick o' my
job! If it paid well, mebbe I wouldn't mind, but they're so
thunderin' stingy round here they don't leave anything de-
cent out for you to take from 'em, yet you're riskin' your
liberty 'n' reputation jest the same. Countin' the poor
pickins 'n' the time I lose in jail I might most 's well be
done with it 'n' work out by the day, as the folks want me
to. I'd make 'bout as much, and I don't know's it would be
any harder!

He could see Rebecca stepping down from the platform, while his own red-haired daughter stood up on her
bench waving her hat with one hand, her handkerchief
with the other, and stamping with both feet.

Now a man sitting beside the mayor rose from his
chair, and Abner heard him call, "Three cheers for the
women who made the flag!"

"Hip, hip, hurrah!"

"Three cheers for the state of Maine!"

"Hip, hip, hurrah!"

"Three cheers for the girl that saved the flag from the
hands of the enemy!"

"Hip, hip, hurrah! Hip, hip, hurrah!"

It was the minister, Mr. Baxter, whose full, vibrant
voice was of the sort to move a crowd. His words rang out
into the clear air and were carried from lip to lip. Hands
clapped, feet stamped, hats swung, while the loud hurrahs

might almost have wakened the echoes on distant Mt. Washington.

The tall, loose-jointed man sat down in the wagon suddenly and took up his reins. "They're gettin' a mite personal, and I guess it's about time for you to be goin' Simpson!" The tone was jocular, but the red mustaches drooped, and the half-hearted cut of his reins he gave to start the white mare on her homeward journey showed that he was not in his usual devil-may-care mood.

"Durn his skin!" he burst out in a vindictive undertone as the mare swung into her long gait. "It's a lie! I thought 'twas somebody's wash! I hain't no enemy!"

While the crowd at the raising dispersed in happy family groups to their picnics in the woods, while the Statue of Liberty, Uncle Sam, and the proud states lunched grandly in the Saco Valley Grange Hall next door to the church with distinguished guests and scarred veterans, the lonely man drove and drove and drove through silent woods and sleepy villages, never alighting to replenish his stock of swapping material. That afternoon he reached a miserable shanty on the edge of a pond.

The faithful wife with the sad mouth and the habitual look of anxiety in her faded eyes came to the door at the sound of wheels and hooves and went doggedly to the horse shed to help him unharness. "You didn't expect to see me back today, did ye?" he asked satirically. "Leastwise not with this same horse? Well, I'm here! You needn't be scairt to look under the wagon seat. There hain't nothin' there, not even my supper, so I hope you're happy for once! No, I guess I hain't goin' to be an angel right away, neither. There wa'nt nawthin' but flags layin' round loose down Riverboro way, 'n' whatever they say, I hain't such a hound as to steal a flag!"

&ð&   &ð&   &ð&

It was natural that young Riverboro should have red, white, and blue dreams on the night after the new flag was raised. A stranger thing, perhaps, is that Abner Simpson should lie down on his hard bed with the flutter of bunting before his eyes and a whirl of unaccustomed words in his mind: *"For it's your star, my star, all our stars together."*

I'm sick of going it alone, he thought. *I guess I'll try the other road for a spell.* And with that he fell asleep.

28

GRAY DAYS AND GOLD

W hen Rebecca looked back upon the years that followed her arrival in Riverboro, she could see only
certain milestones rising in the quiet pathway of the
months.

One major milestone was a Christmas Day at the brick
house. It was a fresh, crystal morning, with icicles hanging
like dazzling pendants from the trees and a glaze of pale
blue on the surface of the snow. The Saco, newly frozen in
the crystal clear night that followed the snowstorm of the
day before, gleamed silver through the barren elms and
maples that bordered the brick house's broad acres.

Rebecca had been busy for weeks before, trying to
make a present for each of the seven persons at Sunnybrook Farm, a somewhat difficult proceeding on an ex-
penditure of fifty cents, hoarded by incredible care. Success had been achieved, however, and the precious packet
had been sent by post two days previous.

Aunt Jane had made Rebecca the loveliest dress of
green cashmere, a soft, soft green like that of a young leaf.
It was very simply made, but the color delighted the eye.
Then there was a beautiful tatting collar from her mother,
some scarlet mittens from Mrs. Cobb, and a handkerchief

from Emma Jane. Miss Miranda had bought her niece a nice gray squirrel muff and scarf, which was even more becoming, if possible, than Rebecca's other articles of wearing apparel. Aunt Miranda's apparent stinginess was honest frugality, Rebecca had learned. Though Miranda still rarely spent money on herself, from the example of Emma Jane's parents she at last had learned that girls do like stylish clothing and it may even do a girl good to supply her a nice outfit from time to time.

Rebecca herself had fashioned an elaborate tea doily with a letter *M* in outline stitch, and a pretty frilled pincushion marked with a *J*, for her two aunts, so that taken all together the day would have been an unequivocal success had nothing else happened; but something else did.

There was a knock at the door at breakfast time, and Rebecca, answering it, was asked by a boy if Miss Rebecca Randall lived there. On being told that she did, he handed her a parcel bearing her name, a parcel which she took like one in a dream and bore into the dining room.

"It's a present; it must be," she said, looking at it, "but I can't think who it could be from."

"A good way to find out would be to open it," remarked Aunt Miranda.

The parcel being untied proved to have two smaller packages within, and Rebecca opened with trembling fingers the one addressed to her. Anybody's fingers would have trembled. There was a case which, when the cover was lifted, disclosed a long chain of delicate pink coral beads — a chain ending in a cross made of coral rosebuds. A card with "Merry Christmas from Mr. Aladdin" lay under the cross.

"Of all things!" exclaimed the two old ladies in unison, rising in their seats. "Who sent it?"

"Mr. Ladd," said Rebecca under her breath.

"Adam Ladd! Well, I never! After he sent you that nice lamp last year, 'cause you so kindly earned one for the Simpsons, I was sure he'd forget you. But here's another Christmas and another present!" exclaimed Jane. "What's in the other package?"

It proved to be a silver chain with a blue enamel locket on it, marked for Emma Jane, though with no card or letter.

That added the last touch—to have him remember them both! There was a letter also, which read:

Dear Miss Rebecca Rowena,

My idea of a Christmas present is something entirely unnecessary and useless. I have always noticed when I give this sort of thing that people love it, so I hope I have not chosen wrong for you and your friend. You must wear your chain this afternoon, please, and let me see it on your neck, for I am coming over in my new sleigh to take you for a drive, if your aunts approve. My aunt is still delighted with the soap.

Sincerely your friend,

Adam Ladd

"Well, well!" cried Miss Jane, "isn't that kind of him? He's very fond of children, so Lydia Burnham says. Now eat your breakfast, Rebecca, and after we've done the dishes you can run over to Emma's and give her her chain. What's the matter, child?"

Rebecca's emotions seemed always to be stored in adjoining compartments and continually getting mixed. At this moment, though her joy was too deep for words, her breakfast almost choked her, and at intervals a tear stole furtively down her cheek.

Though she had seen Adam Ladd only briefly a couple of times in the months since he had bought 300 cakes of soap, Rebecca felt a special warmth in her heart whenever his name was mentioned in the village. She had received but one letter from him — no card — written on business stationery and arriving on St. Valentine's Day, but it contained only polite and formal correspondence noting that he had recently been elected to Wareham Academy's board of directors, and expressing pleasure that she and her aunts had chosen that school as a place to further her education.

But secretly Rebecca felt a kinship to this handsome, lonely young man, who like herself had been reared by an aunt.

Mr. Ladd called as he promised, and he made the acquaintance of the aunts, understanding them both in five minutes as well as if he had known them for years. On a footstool near the open fire sat Rebecca, silent and shy, so conscious of her fine Christmas apparel and jewelry and the presence of Aunt Miranda that she could not utter a word. It was one of her "beauty days." Happiness, excitement, the color of the green dress and the touch of lovely pink in the coral necklace had transformed the little black feathered starling for the time being into a bird of grand plumage. Adam Ladd watched her with evident satisfaction.

Then there was the sleigh ride, and Mr. Ladd proved to be a master horseman, as he guided his dapple-gray, steel-shod mare across the frozen meadow, onto the road, then in a burst of speed raced through the village and into the brick house's curving drive, where he handed down Rebecca from the sleigh with a dapper gallantry that would have thrilled even the most jaded and sophisticated of Boston's society ladies. During the ride, Rebecca had finally found her tongue, and she chattered like any magpie, and so ended that glorious Christmas Day.

Rebecca had finally found her tongue, and she chattered away like any magpie.

Many and many a night thereafter did Rebecca go to sleep with the precious coral chain under her pillow, one hand always upon it to be certain that it was safe. In her dreams, she often dashed wildly in the cutter through field and forest — forests which became the enchanted woods of her books about worlds she had never visited, and the sleigh's ordinary buffalo robe became a robe of magnificent mink.

There had been a more recent milestone in Rebecca's life, a sad one, marking another grave under the willow tree at Sunnybrook Farm. Mira, the baby of the Randall family, died, and Rebecca went home for a two-week visit. The sight of the small, still shape that had been sister Mira, the baby who had been her special charge from her birth until she had taken her leave to live at the brick house, woke into being a host of new thoughts for Rebecca. It is sometimes the mystery of death that brings one to a consciousness of the still greater mystery of life.

It was a sorrowful homecoming for Rebecca. The death of Mira, the sadness of her mother, the loneliness of their little house on a country crossroad, and the pinching economies that went on within it, all worked together to depress Rebecca's sensitive spirit.

Hannah seemed to have grown into a woman during the years of Rebecca's absence. There had always been a strange, unchildlike air about Hannah, but in certain ways she now appeared older than Aunt Jane — soberer and more settled. She was pretty, though in a colorless fashion — pretty and capable.

Rebecca walked through all the old playgrounds and favorite haunts of her early childhood. She visited all her familiar, secret places. Though the woods were frozen, she easily found the spot where the Indian pipes grew in spring, the particular bit of marshy ground where the fringed gentians were largest and bluest in summer, the rock maple where she had once found an oriole's nest, the snow-filled hedge where the field mice had lived, the moss-covered stump where the white toadstools sprung up as if by magic, the hole at the root of the old pine where an ancient and honorable toad had once made his home.

These were the landmarks of her childhood, and she looked at them as across an immeasurable distance, a distance grown long as at the brick house Rebecca had progressed from childhood to the threshold of young womanhood.

Dear little Sunnybrook, the stream that had been her chief companion after her brothers and sisters, was sorry company at this season. There was now no laughing water sparkling in the sunshine. In summer the merry brook had danced over white pebbles on its way to deep pools where it could be still as if it were thinking before rushing on its way to the sea. Now, like Mira, Sunnybrook was cold and quiet, wrapped in its shroud of snow.

But Rebecca knelt by the brink, and putting her ear to the glaze of ice, she fancied where it used to be deepest, that she could hear a faint, tinkling sound. It was all right! Sunnybrook would sing again in the spring. Mira, she knew, would have her singing time in eternity, for now her soul was safe in Jesus' arms as her little body lay in the earth beneath the new blanket of snow on the hillside shadowed by the weeping willow. Though comforted by this knowledge, Rebecca wept for Mira.

In the course of these lonely rambles Rebecca was ever thinking, thinking of one subject. Hannah had never had a chance, had never been freed from the daily care and work of the farm. She, Rebecca, had enjoyed all the privileges thus far. Life at the brick house had not been by any means a path of roses, but there had been the comfort and the companionship of other Riverboro children, as well as chances for study and reading. Riverboro had not been the world itself, but it had been a glimpse of it through a tiny peephole that was infinitely broader than her mother's little farm.

Rebecca shed more than one quiet tear before she could trust herself to offer up as a sacrifice the life which she so much desired to keep for herself, a life from which once she had tried so hard to flee. One morning as her visit neared its end, she plunged into the subject boldly and said, "Hannah, after this spring's school term I'm going to stay at home and let you go away. Aunt Miranda has always wanted you, and it's only fair you should have your turn. Our aunts plan to send me to Wareham Academy, but I think I shall come home to Sunnybrook, instead."

Hannah was darning stockings, and she threaded her needle and snipped off the yarn before she answered, "No thank you, Becky. Mother couldn't do without me, and I hate going to school. I can read and write and cipher as well as anybody now, and that's enough for me. I'd rather die than teach school for a living.

"The winter'll go fast," Hannah continued, "for Will Melville is going to lend me his mother's sewing machine, and I'm going to make white petticoats out of the piece of muslin Aunt Jane sent and have 'em just solid with tucks. Then there's going to be a singing school and a social circle in Temperance after New Year's. I shall have a real good time now I'm grown up. I'm not one to be lonesome, Becky," Hannah ended with a warm blush. "I love this place."

With a quiet smile Hannah opened a thimble box in her sewing basket and pulled forth a gleaming object she slipped on the third finger of her left hand. "I've kept this hidden, Becky, since we're in mourning for Mira," she said quietly. "But I want *you* to know."

"Will Melville?" Rebecca's eyes grew wide as she saw the ring, a gold band, unadorned except for a modest diamond.

"Yes. We went to Lewiston together two weeks ago, and Will bought it for me with money he had saved from selling a steer."

"When . . . have you set a date?"

"I'll be seventeen this summer. Mother says I can marry on my birthday." Hannah's eyes were full of merry pleasure as the sisters embraced each other. Glee gave way to happy tears as Hannah and Rebecca hugged.

The short train ride from Temperance to Maplewood to catch the stagecoach to Riverboro next morning gave Rebecca time to clear her brain. Glad as she was that Hannah was soon to be a bride, *I've got more living to do,* she told herself, *than to marry at seventeen.* Rebecca laughed aloud as she realized that Aunt Miranda, for once, would agree with her sensible statement.

ABOUT
THE AUTHORS

E ric E. Wiggin, 51, is a native of Maine and has been a country pastor and school teacher in his home state. He now lives with his wife, Dorothy (Dot), and their youngest child, Bradstreet, as a country gentleman in rural Fruitport, Michigan, near where Dot spent her girlhood.

Wiggin has also been a college English instructor, and currently is the editor of contemporary versions of Harvey's *Grammars,* first published in 1868 as companions to McGuffey's *Eclectic Readers.* Wiggin contributes regularly to such periodicals as *Moody Monthly, Confident Living, Power for Living,* and *World.* He and Dot are the parents of four children — two of them born in Maine — and two grandchildren.

ช. ช. ช.

Kate Douglas Wiggin (nee Smith, 1856-1923) was born in Philadelphia. As a child she moved with her mother and sister to Portland, Maine, near her mother's birthplace. Kate became a founder of the American school kindergarten movement.

Kate Wiggin's books include *Rebecca of Sunnybrook Farm* (1903) and *New Chronicles of Rebecca* (1906). It is on these two volumes that Books I and II of the present *Rebecca* series are based.

The typeface for the text of this book is *Times Roman*. In 1930, typographer Stanley Morison joined the staff of *The Times* (London) to supervise design of a typeface for the reformatting of this renowned English daily. Morison had overseen type-library reforms at Cambridge University Press in 1925, but this new task would prove a formidable challenge despite a decade of experience in paleography, calligraphy, and typography. *Times New Roman* was credited as coming from Morison's original pencil renderings in the first years of the 1930s, but the typeface went through numerous changes under the scrutiny of a critical committee of dissatisfied *Times* staffers and editors. The resulting typeface, *Times Roman*, has been called the most used, most successful typeface of this century. The design is of enduring value to English and American printers and publishers, who choose the typeface for its readability and economy when run on today's high-speed presses.

Substantive Editing:
Michael Hyatt

Copy Editing:
Susan Kirby

Cover Design:
Steve Diggs & Friends
Nashville, Tennessee

Page Composition:
Xerox Ventura Publisher
Printware 720 IQ Laser Printer

Printing and Binding:
Maple-Vail Book Manufacturing Group
York, Pennsylvania

Cover Printing:
Strine Printing Company
York, Pennsylvania